SHEENA CUNDY

Bonkers and Broomsticks

A Witch Lit Novel

First published by Treehouse Magic 2019

First edition

This book was professionally typeset on Reedsy.
Find out more at reedsy.com

For my dear Mum.

You're mad, bonkers, completely off your head, but I'll tell you a secret...all the best people are.

LEWIS CARROLL - ALICE IN WONDERLAND

Contents

Acknowledgement

Gratitude to my beta readers: Ruth Aitken, Wendy Steele, Portland Jones, Elizabeth Bayliss, Sue Leary and Jennifer Wilson, who helped to make this a better book.
And to Mr. C for proofreading at the eleventh hour...missing that pre-order deadline just wasn't an option.

1

Libido Lost

Minerva had been watching the two pigeons copulating on the bird table for long enough. 'Damn you Spring,' she cried out loud, 'How dare you raise your ugly, phallic head and so rudely remind me that sex is indeed the order of the season. Talk about rubbing salt into a wound!'

A hot blooded female to the core, Minerva prided herself on being totally at one with her inner sex goddess. Pleasure and passion were her life blood, flowing through her veins and out of her flaming red hair. She was a woman on fire. Or at least, she had been until now.

Everyone was at it, apart from her and David. She thought about her missing sex drive and wondered where exactly it had driven off to, certainly not in her faithful old Mr. Morris; it wouldn't get far that's for sure. She thought about the reason for its departure and blamed it on the dreaded men-o-whats-it disease. Volcanic, hot flushes and murderous tendencies she could put up with as long as she could still be a woman where it really mattered. In the bedroom.

What had become of her? She was a frigid and fading shadow of her former self, left wondering where the rest of her had gone. Not wanting to resign herself to a life of misery without it, she was determined to find this wild and primal part of who she was and put it back where it belonged.

Perhaps she needed some security in her life.

Did Witches marry vicars? The idea of being restricted by rules of any kind was enough to put her off marrying anyone let alone a vicar. But David was different. He didn't seem to mind who or what she was and in a two-people-of-very-different backgrounds sort of way, Minerva and David were living proof that it can work. Did it really matter if someone was into God and the bible or a Goddess and her magic? Weren't they just a man and a woman when you stripped it all down? But this, thought Minerva, was the problem. Nakedness was not something that had the same effect on her anymore. In fact, it had no effect at all. Such a painful loss was becoming harder to hide, but she couldn't fake it forever. She couldn't pretend she was in heaven when it felt like hell. She had to do something...and as the beginnings of an idea began to form in her mind, she hurried to the greenhouse, grabbed an empty seed packet and began to scribble furiously over the faded print:

My lost Libido's safe return
As flames of passion ever burn
Sexual power sets me free
As I will, so mote it be!

Chanting the words as she wrote them, a bubble of excitement from inside Minerva began to heat up and radiate around her body. It was encouraging. She loved the immediate effect magic had on the system, and smiling to herself, she folded the paper carefully into quarters and tucked it down her cleavage. Then, from out of nowhere and much to her annoyance, Rod Stewart strutted across the screen of her mind. She'd never liked him much. But there he was in those ridiculous leopard skin leggings, blurting out, *'Do you think I'm Sexy'* in that irritating, gravelly voice and before she knew it she was humming the wretched tune while making her way to the far end of the garden.

* * *

On such a warm and glorious day, no one could blame Lucifer for sunning himself right in the middle of the herb patch. The soft pile of chamomile was the perfect spot for a cat nap.

'Oh Lucifer, I might have known…sometimes I think you do it on purpose – anything to make me work harder for what I want!' Minerva bent over the sleeping cat and reached for the lavender behind him, her long silver chain and pentacle brushing over his body. The startled animal sprang into action hissing furiously; claws open and and teeth bared.

'Argh!' screamed Minerva as the wild creature grabbed her by the great mass of hair and began to kick like a frantic rabbit against her head.

Not surprisingly, the louder the screams, the harder the cat fought as he battled to preserve his place in the herb patch and Minerva held on for dear life to her hair. Having so much of it certainly saved her from the scratches of those great claws, although her hands and arms didn't escape so lightly. Blood oozed everywhere and to top it all, she lost her balance, caught her foot on the concrete statue of Hecate and fell against the wheelbarrow beside it. Only when Minerva toppled *into* the wheelbarrow, did Lucifer release himself and bolt into the back field; his catnap brought to a premature end.

* * *

After an unresponsive welcome at the front of Crafty Cottage, Isis let herself in through the back gate. It was a disturbing scene for someone as easily traumatized as Isis. And although she was getting better at coping with the unexpected - it happened a lot to Minerva – blood, she would never get used to.

'Oh my word! What's happened?!' screeched Isis, her eyes darting around furiously for the murderer.

Hearing the mumbled cries from the other side of the garden, she ran across to the scene of the crime where she found Minerva, clutching her head and crumpled up in the wheelbarrow. Her hair clung to her face and the blood on her arms sparkled like fresh paint in the sun. Isis froze.

'The *bastard*,' groaned Minerva. 'Did you see him? Where did he go?'

'Who? What did he do to you Minerva?'

'What does it look like?' she threw her hands up, 'Wait till I get hold of the beast!'

'Oh no, you mustn't do that, Minerva! It's best to call the police, straight away!'

She darted through the back door and came out almost immediately with the phone in her hand, tapping at it furiously.

'NO ISIS!' Minerva hauled herself out of the wheelbarrow and lunged at Isis to grab the phone. 'It's not a police matter.'

'What do you mean it's not a police matter? You were attacked!'

'Yes, by Lucifer! He was the one who attacked me!'

'The cat?'

'Yes! That god forsaken fallen angel of a damn cat!'

Minerva was exasperated to say the least. As if her ordeal wasn't bad enough without Isis getting the wrong end of the stick, which happened a lot. She sat on the back step with her head in her hands, while Isis pulled up a chair from the patio and the two of them sat in silence staring at the crazy paving.

'Where is he now?' said Isis. 'And what actually happened?'

'Oh he's buggered off into the back field,' said Minerva. 'He's not daft and if he's got any sense he'll wait a good while before he comes back. What happened? Well, I had an idea for a spell… and with Beltane almost upon us it's the perfect time for magic of a certain kind if you get my meaning?' Minerva cast a sideways glance at Isis while pulling out straggling weeds from the cracks in the concrete.

'Oh,' said Isis, fidgeting.

'I had my eye on the lavender for an under-garment pouch,' said Minerva wistfully, 'which of course, was right at the back of the herb patch behind Lucifer. I should've known better, but you know how it is Isis, when the mood takes me…'

'Yes, Minerva, I know how it is, or at least I think I do…'

Minerva knew if there was only one good thing that awful sleaze bag of a husband, Derek, had ever done in his miserable excuse for a life; it was to leave his wife. Isis may have been blinded at the time but Minerva was certain she had now regained her senses enough to realize the awful Molly Maid had actually done her a huge favour. Seducing the weak and pathetic Derek into running away from his marriage was actually the best thing to happen to Isis for twenty years. Anyone could see that.

'I think I'm finally doing what you said I would,' said Isis, sitting up straighter.

Minerva was busy inspecting her bloody scratches, 'And what was that...?'

'Stepping into my power! You used to say it all the time when Derek first left.'

'Ah well, I always knew you would! You just needed time to *detoxify* that's all. Stepping into your power would never have happened with Derek around to cramp your style. Thank the Goddess that awful stain of a man is out of your life - wiped away by the most helpful of Molly Maids - what a thoroughly good job she did.'

Isis turned to Minerva, 'You're absolutely right, and I've never felt as good in ages. Even the panic attacks are getting less now.'

'I had noticed, yes,' said Minerva, 'although I think I may have given you a bit of a turn just then.' She nodded at the wheelbarrow lying on its side and turned to her friend, 'Isis... I have an idea.'

'Does it involve magic by any chance?'

'You know me too well,' said Minerva. 'It's about something which has gone missing...a temporary loss, I hope.'

She reached down her sweaty cleavage and pulled out the damp and crumpled seed packet. Isis read the spell and the words on the other side: *Wanted - One missing Libido.*

Isis cleared her throat, 'Is that what I think it is?'

'And what would that be..?'

'You know...' said Isis pushing her tilting hairpiece a bit too far the other way. 'Oh Minerva, stop it! You know I find the subject *difficult* to say the least. It's never been easy for me.'

'That makes two of us at the moment, then!' scoffed Minerva. 'If you must know, I'm beside myself with it, or should I say *lack of it* at the moment. Goddess knows I'm doing a good job for now but there's only so much faking a woman can do!'

'I never thought I'd hear you say it,' said Isis. 'Is it anything to do with the men-o-whats-it thing? How long has it been missing?'

'I fear it's part of this awful *condition,* yes. And it's been gone for far too long,' said Minerva running her hands through matted clumps of hair. 'It's like having the rug pulled very sharply from under one's feet.'

Isis looked serious, 'Or in your case, the duvet ripped off the bed...'

'That, Isis, is a far more accurate analogy!' said Minerva. 'But sadly it doesn't make up for the pain of such a loss. Can you imagine it?'

'I don't have to Minerva,' said Isis, looking down at her sandals.

'Ah yes...' said Minerva. 'You know exactly how it feels because yours has been missing too!'

'Yes, you could say that,' said Isis. 'And for longer than I care to remember.'

'You what?' Minerva could hardly contain her disgust, 'Twenty years of marriage and no sex at all? Nothing?'

Isis looked shocked, 'Well not quite, but almost...Derek wasn't that sort of man I suppose.'

'Oh I see,' said Minerva, 'and what about you? What about *your* needs? How bloody selfish of him! What sort of man doesn't want sex and worse still denies the pleasure of such a wonderful thing to the woman who has given her life, *sacrificed* her life in fact...'

'Minerva, you're making it sound worse than it was.'

'How can anything be worse than a non-existent sex life?'

'Well, in a loveless marriage it's what happens I suppose,' said Isis, her voice breaking, 'You don't really think about something if it's not there in the first place.'

Minerva put her arm around her friend and squeezed the skinny shoulders. How fragile she felt. 'Isis, I feel your pain, really I do. Sympathy won't help and pity is the last thing you need but you have my empathy. Welcome to the club, although our situations *are* different. The missing link in your case is a man, and in mine... it's the *urge.* Now shall we move on and actually do something about solving this problem rather than dwelling on it?'

'You're probably right,' said Isis. 'Let's get on with it.'

'Right, that's all I needed to hear,' said Minerva, getting up and brushing herself down. 'First, things first...my spell book, and some sort of beverage for recharging the batteries, medicinal of course.'

Isis followed her friend back into the house with a twinge of apprehension accompanied by the smallest glimmer of excitement. She felt for her wobbling hairpiece and nudged it back to centre.

Perhaps magic wasn't such a bad idea.

* * *

Ronnie marched along behind the buggy, glimpsing at the sleeping passenger with a sense of relief. Playgroup had worn her out nicely and hopefully she would sleep for a while, although her doting grandmother often had the opposite effect on the two-year old for some reason. She checked her mobile for the time, and picked up the pace to Crafty Cottage. Parking the buggy on the patio round the back and checking to see that her daughter was still sleeping, she made her way inside.

'Hello darling.' Minerva beamed at her from behind the pages of a huge book, 'What brings you home so soon? No 'mother's coffee morning' today? It *is* on a Tuesday isn't it?'

'No, I mean yes… it *is* today but I'm not going,' said Ronnie, throwing her baby bag down on the sofa.

'But you're going somewhere, I can tell. And is that with or without Morrigan?' said Minerva, walking out to the patio.

'No Mum, please! Don't wake her, she's asleep and with a bit of luck will stay that way for a while. I'm off to see Joe, actually… You wouldn't mind keeping an eye on her would you?'

'No of course not,' said Isis, jumping up from the sofa. 'We can do that, or I can do that if your mother gets busy.'

'I'm sure we'll cope,' said Minerva. 'Just a bit of unfinished business to attend to first haven't we Isis?'

'If you say so,' said Isis, tentatively walking towards the buggy. 'I know what I'd rather be doing though.'

'You do seem to have a way with her Isis, you both do,' said Ronnie shooting a quick glance at her mother.

'Nice of you to say so darling,' purred Minerva. 'And yes, clearly you do have a thing with babies, Isis. Perhaps you need one of your own?'

Isis turned beetroot and walked out of the room, 'Shall I put the kettle on?' she called from the kitchen.

'Mum, you're the devil incarnate sometimes,' said Ronnie.

'Isis is much stronger than you think,' said Minerva, putting the spell book down as the cry from the patio reached them.

Ronnie looked at the face of the Green Man clock on the wall, 'Mum, I've got to go, I won't be *too* long.'

She gave Minerva a quick peck on the cheek and darted out of the room, checking the mirror in the hallway, 'Bye you two, have fun!'

Isis returned with two steaming cups to an empty room and saw Minerva bent over the buggy and a screaming Morrigan.

'I swear this child is a banshee in disguise,' said Minerva, lifting the noisy infant and planting a kiss on her hot cheeks. But this did nothing to pacify her granddaughter who continued to scream while Minerva looked helplessly at Isis.

'Give her here,' said Isis, with outstretched arms. 'Why don't you carry on with your research, Minerva?'

'Well, now you mention it...' said Minerva. 'We need to focus on our strengths don't you think? That child does seem to respond to your more *genteel* ways.'

It was a fair swap. The change was instant as Minerva took the spell book and all screaming stopped as Isis bounced and rocked Morrigan around the room in her arms.

'I have to say, Isis, you have the magic touch when it comes to calming the stormy seas of my raging granddaughter,' said Minerva, drawing her spectacles down from the top of her head and opening the spell book.

'I've always loved babies,' said Isis, continuing to walk up and down. 'Pity Derek didn't, but maybe there might be someone else who does if I'm ever lucky enough to find him.'

Minerva chuckled, 'Have no doubt about it, my friend, you *will* find him. But luck is far too random a commodity and can't be relied on. Magic is a much safer bet in my book!'
Isis didn't know whether to be scared or happy. Either way, she was pretty sure it wouldn't affect the outcome. Not if she

knew Minerva.

2

Freya's Return

Ronnie felt an odd twinge of guilt at having some time to herself for once. It was strange walking without the buggy and the sing-song chatter of her daughter chirping away in front of her. Although having a baby had been a shock, she couldn't imagine life without her now; she worried about losing the people she loved more than anything. It was hardly surprising after Bob had left the earthly shores for the great stable in the sky. He may only have been a horse, but he'd meant the world to Ronnie.

How did one get used to gaining a baby so quickly after the loss of a dear friend like Bob? Numbed by pain, she had barely lived through those heartbreaking first few months. But somehow she'd done it, found a strength she didn't know existed and got through the early days.

'Time is a great healer,' her mother had said and if the last eighteen months were anything to go by, she was right. Ronnie's newly appointed role of motherhood had left no time to dwell on the past, and slowly the weight of it had lifted; replaced by the blessing which accompanies all new life and

the love which grows out of it.

Enjoying her freedom, she breathed in deeply and quickened her step along the narrow pavement, spurred on by the thought of seeing Joe.

He'd said midday hadn't he? But why at the marina she had no idea as she cast her mind back to the phone call earlier…

'Can you meet me later at work, Ron, that's if you're not doing anything?'

'I'll try, shall I get Mum to have Morrigan?

'That'd be good if you can manage it…'

Ronnie waited for him to explain but he didn't.

'What is it then?' she asked after a long pause.

He laughed, 'Ah well, that'd be telling now wouldn't it?'

'Oh Joe don't,' she narrowed her eyes at the phone in her hand. 'Tell me…'

'If you can get down here for one-ish, you'll see for yourself,' he said playfully, 'I'll tell you one thing though Ron – you'll love it, I know you will!'

'Why do you do this to me? You know I hate being kept in suspense.'

A wicked chuckle rippled across the air waves, 'Oh really? Could've fooled me! How about trying a bit of patience, just for a few hours eh? Must go… I'll see you later, yeah?'

She sighed, 'Okay then…bye.'

He was right, patience wasn't one of her virtues but she did love surprises. And the best ones were worth waiting for weren't they?

Reaching the marina at last, she scanned the boatyard for Joe, her eyes darting between the boats on the hard standing and those in the water. The tide was up and boats of all shapes and sizes bobbed around like corks in the bright sunshine. She'd forgotten her sunglasses and dazzled by the light, she squinted to get a better view but couldn't see him anywhere.

'Ron! Over here!'

Tilting her head to gauge the direction of his voice, she saw him down on the pontoons, one arm raised to the sky. Waving back, she smiled and made her way down the wooden steps onto the floating path of the pontoon, as close to walking on water as it gets. Joe was casually leaning on a post, a squashed pack of tobacco balanced on one knee, carefully pinching the small brown clumps onto a white flapping piece of paper. 'Hi Ron,' he said, without looking up, 'Are you ready then?'

'I'm here aren't I?'

'You certainly are,' said Joe lighting his roll-up, 'And so is this beauty….' he turned around to the boat behind him, much longer than any of the surrounding ones, 'What do you think?'

'What do you mean?' she searched his face and the boat for clues.

He straightened up and stepped backwards to touch the peeling paintwork, 'This, Ron, is our new home, courtesy of none other than my colleague and our old departed friend…Ropey, God rest his soul.'

He walked alongside the boat and signalled her to follow him, 'Meet Freya's Return, Ropey's gaff before he returned to the halls of the great Valhalla…' he looked at Ronnie's puzzled face, 'It's ours Ron, he left it to me, *to us*. That's if you're interested of course.'

Ronnie stopped, 'Ropey left you his home?'

'That's right, I got it in writing yesterday from the executor of his will. He didn't have any family, remember?'

She did remember, yes. 'He thought the world of you Joe, I'm not surprised he left you his prized possession.' She stared at him, 'What are you going to do with it?'

'What do you think I'm going to do? I'm going to live on it,' he said without taking his eyes off it, 'Care to join me? You and Morrigan?'

She stared at him, at the boat and back again, 'Are you serious?' Both of us? You really mean that?'

'Why wouldn't I? You come as a package don't you?'
He cocked his head to one side and fixed his twinkly eyes on her, 'Come on board and have a look first, see what you think...'

'What kind of a boat is this?' said Ronnie, following him.

'A Dutch barge is what she is,' Joe called back, climbing aboard, 'and Ropey loved her. Sailed her all the way back from Holland years ago...long before I knew him. He worked here for years, and as far back as I can remember, this is where he lived.'

Joe reached for her hand and held her steady as she stepped onto the boat from the wobbling pontoon. She paused to stare at the fading picture of a voluptuous golden-haired woman above the double doors of the cabin.

'Freya?'

'I think so, yeah, some kind of Goddess I reckon...'

'Norse I think, if my memory serves me right.'

A childhood full of myth and magic was certain to leave particular imprints in the mind and Ronnie's was full of all kinds of Gods and Goddesses. She remembered gazing with wonder at the glossy illustrations in one favourite book which she'd return to again and again – mesmerized by the images of beautiful women of all shapes and sizes, usually in various stages of undress...a bit like this one.

'That's right, you'd know wouldn't you Ron?' Joe laughed, 'You don't grow up with a mother like Minerva without picking up a fair bit of *mystical* knowledge eh? What's Freya all about then?' He nodded to the fading paintwork, 'If I know Ropey, my guess is that she's some kind of fertility or sex Goddess, am I right?'

He looked uncannily like a pirate, she thought. His shoulder length wavy hair held back with both hands to reveal not one but two silver earrings glinting in the sun. He widened his casual stance and continued to gaze upon the scantily clad Goddess, slowly returning his gaze to Ronnie, 'Not a bad old girl is she?'

Her heart pounded against her ribcage. Why did he do this to her? She felt like a girl all over again and although motherhood had claimed her prematurely she still felt like a maiden. She stared at the Goddess above her, 'A warrior Goddess I think.'

'That would be the Vikings then wouldn't it?' said Joe looking at the faded and peeling paint. 'That's some cloak she's got on isn't it? Plenty of feathers, but not much else from what I can see! And that's a rare old chariot she's riding with a right pair of beasts at the front there.'

'They're cats,' said Ronnie, 'And that necklace she's wearing was made by dwarves, so the story goes... The Necklace of Brisingamen I think it's called.'

She made a note to look up more about her. It wouldn't be hard to find in her mother's library at home. Minerva had quite a collection of magical books and Freya was sure to be somewhere among them. But right now she was riding across this old Dutch barge and Ronnie felt a cold shiver run down the back of her legs. It wasn't unfamiliar and yet it startled her. She looked around for any other signs.

'What's the matter Ron?' said Joe, 'Don't tell me the Viking woman's scaring you?'

'No. Just makes me feel a bit weird that's all.'

'What sort of weird? Weird ghostly or weird as in ill? You've gone a bit white looking.'

'It's that same feeling I get when someone's not around anymore…' her voice trailed off and her eyes wandered to the water.

'You mean dead,' Joe lowered his voice and looked behind him, 'Maybe Ropey's still about eh? It kind of makes sense I suppose. Why wouldn't the old boy still want to be looking out for his boat?'

'And you, Joe,' whispered Ronnie, 'He'd be looking out for you too.'

Joe gave her one of his rare and serious looks, 'Well if that's the case, I don't mind that at all. He always looked out for me here, what with the water being a wild beast as he used to say… I always felt safe when he was around, especially in the early days when I was learning the ropes.' He smiled at the thought. 'Good old Ropey, he was a bloody good friend to me.'

'I know he was,' said Ronnie touching his arm, 'And I'm pretty sure he'll continue to be.' She cast her eyes around the boat, 'Are you going to show me round then? I'd like to see where I'm moving to!'

Joe grabbed her and hugged her tight. 'Come on then,' he said, taking her hand and opening the small double doors into the living room. A wood burning stove sat in the far corner of a small room littered with boating magazines, empty mugs and biscuit wrappers. She looked closer at an old woollen jumper squashed between the cushion and the back of a worn armchair and saw it was covered in white hair.

'Where's the cat?' she said glancing around.

'Christ, I'd forgotten about her!' said Joe. 'She was always a bit wild anyway...probably gone walkabout. You know what these feral cats are like.'

'What are you going to do about the dogs? They're not used to cats! Oh Joe, do you reckon it's going to be too much...it's such a small space.'

Joe laughed, 'It'll be cosy won't it? Good fun for all of us I'd say. The dogs? Well, they'll get used to the cat if she's still here that is...animals sort their pecking order out in their own time if you leave them to it.'

'That's what I'm worried about,' said Ronnie. She turned to Joe, who had disappeared into the next room, and followed him in.

'Aaaargh!' Joe jumped back, clutching his chest as a hissing cat sprang to the floor, ears flattened and teeth bared. When it saw Ronnie, it made itself as tall as it could and the hissing became a low growl.

'Jesus!' said Ronnie hiding behind Joe.

The wild creature was a ball of dirty white and matted fur. She was not in the least bit scared of them and continued to hiss and spit, claws gripped tight to the old armchair in the corner.

'Maybe you shouldn't have disturbed her!'

'How the hell did I know she was there,' said Joe sucking his bloody hand. 'She's the one who's disturbed, look what she did to me!'

The cat flew out of the room leaving the pair glaring at each other.

'Where's she gone? Can she get off the boat?' said Ronnie.

'Let's go and have a look,' Joe gingerly walked through the narrow corridors, 'She went this way didn't she?'

Ronnie had a sinking feeling as images of wild cats and dogs, snarling teeth and flying fur came into her mind. And a toddler. The thought of a two year old as well in such a small space, on a boat surrounded by water and a wobbly pontoon filled her with horror.

'Joe,' she bit her lip nervously, 'what about Morrigan?'

Joe sat down on a rickety chair, still hanging onto his hand and peered at her beneath waves of golden brown hair, 'Ron,' he said quietly, 'your daughter is made of strong stuff like you. It'll be a great life here on the boat. And the animals? Just a few teething problems that's all. We can manage or at least I can if you can.'

She sighed, wanting to believe him. 'I'll try, really I will but you can understand my concern can't you? Morrigan's only a baby, really'.

'Not for much longer Ron,' said Joe putting his arm around her, 'Stop worrying! And you know what?'

'What?'

He squeezed her shoulders, jumped up and made for the door, 'Worse things have happened at sea...ask Freya!

Yeah, she thought, I might just do that.

3

Prickly News

Minerva's missing libido problem was proving hard to solve. Having spent a whole afternoon scanning every spell book she had – of which there was a multitude – she still couldn't find what she was looking for. It was ludicrous.

She could feel herself getting more and more worked up the further she delved into the mysteries of researching such an elusive subject. There seemed to be every kind of magic for romance which was fine if that's what you were after. But it wasn't much use to her, especially at the moment. The insatiable hunger for the joys of the flesh had disappeared completely and she was sure it would take more than a few rose petals and Cupid's arrows to bring it back.

Determined to find it somehow, she was convinced *somewhere* there was some way of leading her from the cold and lonely shadows of a passionless existence back to the burning flames of a healthy sex life.

With a full Beltane moon looming, she knew it was the perfect time for this very important piece of magical solo work...but she needed answers and she needed them fast. It was all very well for Isis. They'd managed to put together a particularly effective spell for her, tried and tested by Minerva to get the relationship she wanted. Particularly as it had worked in no time with the handsome vicar. This was the fascinating part of magic as far as Minerva was concerned – as long as you knew what you wanted – anything was possible. Perhaps she was trying too hard? She wondered if it was too early for a tipple and without giving it any more thought, headed for the cupboard where the brandy lived. When the phone rang, without thinking, she answered it.

'Oh hello, is that Mrs Crafty? said a faraway voice. 'It's Prickly Hall here. Your mother is in our care, remember?'

'Yes,' replied Minerva from the inside of the drinks cupboard, 'of course I do. It was hard enough getting her in there...I won't forget that in a hurry!'

She grimaced as the vivid memories came flooding back - such an awful time they'd had of installing her mother into the home - but she was there now, thank the Goddess. She listened to the woman while pouring the amber liquid into a glass. 'What do you mean she's being rude?' said Minerva, 'I don't need you to tell me that! I had a whole childhood, those terrible teenage years and now here I am in middle age where she still continues to do what she's always done... and that is,' Minerva struggled for breath, 'exactly what the hell she likes, so it would help your good selves if you got used to it or more importantly – *her*. I'm afraid my mother is a law unto herself as you are beginning to find out. How long has she been in the home? Hardly two months isn't it?'

She stared at the silent phone and downed the brandy in one shot. After what seemed an age, the faraway voice replied,

'Well Mrs. Crafty, the fact of the matter is, I cannot expect anyone to put up with the constant barrage of verbal abuse from your mother anymore. Not only is it extremely upsetting for the staff but it's not conducive to a caring environment or the people living in it. She is not the *only* resident in the home.'

Was it a hot flush or her hackles rising? Minerva wasn't sure, but there was something about the delivery of the speech which she found extremely annoying. Normally, she would empathize – knowing only too well how awkward and antagonistic her mother could be – but the woman's patronizing tone irritated her.

It wasn't called Prickly Hall for nothing.

She narrowed her eyes and inhaled deeply, 'I must say Mrs. *Prickly*,' she said to the warm mouthpiece in her sweating hand, 'abuse does appear to be rather a strong word but if you say so, it must *be* so, and I bow to your infinite wisdom. No doubt it's an ability you've developed working with the elderly and their foibles over the decades... How long did you say you've been there?'

After a long pause came the reply, 'Two years... nearly.'

'Sorry? I didn't quite get that?'

'I see you have a hearing problem just like your mother,' said the manager.

You bare-faced cheek of a bitch, thought Minerva.

'*And* I have been in the position long enough to know my job, thank you!'

'That's comforting to hear I must say,' said Minerva, 'Now, where were we? Ah yes, my mother. What in fact, are you proposing to do? I'm sure she'll settle down in good time, she is after all, ninety-one you know!'

'This is the problem Mrs. Crafty. We don't have the time

or the space to allow for the level of care required for your mother, unless...'

'Unless what?' spat Minerva down the phone, 'Oh I see where this is going. Are you fishing for more funds? Is she that high maintenance?'

'No. To be quite blunt about it and with regret Mrs. Crafty, you will have to arrange another residential package for your mother. I'm afraid we simply cannot accommodate her any more. She has upset too many people and that's not only the staff - she hurls expletives at the other residents on a regular basis and the complaints from the visitors increases by the day. I have tried to reason with her but there has been no improvement and only deterioration in her manner and behaviour ever since she began her time with us,' said Mrs. Prickly with a heavy sigh.

Minerva felt almost sorry for her, but not quite. 'Are you sure you can kick her out like that?' she said, pouring herself another drink, 'Where will she go? I need some time to find somewhere...'

It didn't bear thinking about.

Cybele Crafty was one of a kind and not for the faint-hearted or lesser mortals as Minerva knew only too well. Throughout her childhood she had been ostrasized for having such a fierce and outspoken mother, leaving the poor young Minerva baffled and heartbroken to have missed out on friendships that could've been and parties that never happened. Such miserable memories were buried under the thick hide she'd grown over time, hidden from view and almost laid to rest. Until now.

'Damn her!' cried Minerva, hurling the phone across the room.

Snatching her Tarot cards she pulled out the first one without bothering to shuffle at all. Justice. 'What are you doing showing up?' she blurted out, looking deeply into it. Staring at the card gave her a sense of mystery and wonder, as if she were looking far into the mists of time. Somewhere beyond the veil the answers lay within her grasp, only just out of view. She sensed an air of karma. All would be revealed she knew, but meanwhile, the lessons of justice were playing out and she was an innocent bystander.

'Not again, please,' she said to the card. Hadn't she put up with enough as far as her mother was concerned? She gave the pack a good shuffle and asked for guidance.

The Empress…the archetypal mother.

Now she was beginning to see the mother daughter relationship right there in her hands. Or more precisely, in her house. Minerva inhaled deeply and pulled one more card. The Four of Swords washed over the enormity of the other two cards and brought some relief in that moment. She allowed the image to speak to her and confirm the balancing of scales and a time of rest and recovery. She smirked at the irony and poured another drink, savouring the liquid fire as it slipped down into her belly. There was nothing quite like it…or her mother.

What was she going to do? Minerva drank until the tension eased and the nerves settled into numbness, until her eyes became heavy and the world hazy. Until a voice in the distance eventually roused her from sleep.

'Minerva.'

She peered through a mouthful of thick red hair and groaned, 'What…who's that?'

'Darling, what's happened? You're upset.'

David knew her too well.

'Not anymore,' she sighed and slowly pulled herself up from

the table, 'You're here.'

'I'll make us a coffee and you can tell me all about it,' said David in hushed tones.

'David,' she muttered, 'I am not a child.'

Bursting into tears was not something Minerva did very often. But her guard was down and her hair stuck like sideburns to her wet cheeks as she almost choked on the angry tears. David was even more of a blur than before.

'Here,' said David, gently pushing a clean handkerchief into her hand.

After a significant amount of nose blowing, hair rearranging and a trip to the toilet, Minerva was glad of the strong coffee and peered at David over the top of her mug.

'Shocks do this you know.'

'Do what?'

'Make one emotional.'

'Clearly something has, although you don't have to justify anything Minerva. Aren't we past all that?' said David, reaching across the table for her hand.

She managed a watery smile while slurping her coffee. Unfortunately, it wasn't a good combination in her wobbly state and the dark, hot liquid splashed onto the Empress. 'Oh no,' winced Minerva, dabbing herself and the card with equal care, 'Just to remind me of course...'

'Minerva, what are you talking about? Is there any chance of us having an anywhere near coherent conversation that makes any sense or do I resign myself to the mystical ramblings and cryptic notions —'

'— of a drunken Witch?'

'Shall we forget that and get back on track?' said David, nodding to the Empress.

What woman could be other than charmed by such a smooth operator?

'It's my mother,' said Minerva, 'they're chucking her out...'

'From the home? She's only just moved in,' David looked puzzled, 'Surely they can't just chuck her out? What's happened?'

'To Prickly Hall? My mother,' said Minerva, 'My mother has *happened* David! Doing what she's best at - antagonizing, annoying, shocking and abusing - those were the words from the horse's mouth...that awful prickly, woman the manager. She called earlier to give me the good news, although hardly from your good book is it?'

'Can we leave out that kind of talk?' said a stern-faced David.

Minerva almost spat out the remains of her coffee, 'Such a wonderful way with words vicar,' she said, looking at David's expressionless face, 'Alas, there is no room at the home anymore. We will have to *'find another residential package elsewhere Mrs Crafty'*. I could've throttled the woman really I could, I'm sure she enjoyed it.'

'I think that's perhaps an exaggeration...'

'No David! I could smell the relief and contempt filtering through the airwaves, honestly. And who can blame her at the end of the day? Believe me, I know better than any man or beast – what my mother can be like or should I say, what she *is* like. I've told you - and you've seen it for yourself when we moved her out of her house and into that place – how perfectly demonic she is, the devil in disguise. Well actually no, there is no disguise...she's the real deal.'

'Well, she *had* lived in that house for sixty years Minerva, you can't really blame her for not wanting to leave her home without a bit of a fight.'

'A bit of a fight?' Minerva said each word slowly and deliberately.

David shifted awkwardly in his chair, 'Well perhaps it would have been less of one if she hadn't barricaded herself in with all those bags.'

'Oh yes,' hissed Minerva, 'You mean the bags of rubbish that she never put out for years but just kept piling up in every room, stinking and rotting - *those bags!* Not to mention the bags of un-used clothes she wouldn't let anyone throw out or take to the charity shop...plus the bags of papers, crockery and you name it - it was in a bag. In fact, I don't know how she didn't leave that house in a bag herself because I can tell you, on more than one occasion it crossed my mind. I don't know what stopped me doing it.'

'I did, if you remember,' said David. 'There is only a fight when there are opposing sides Minerva. You and your mother never stopped. Thankfully, I was there to keep the peace, or at least try to, but thank God we managed it in the end.'

'Yes, and the God at the time was Sidney Squalor and his skip hire firm...' Minerva winced at the memory, 'That wasn't really his name was it?'

'No, the firm was called Squalor Skips...' frowned David, 'At least, I don't think it was *his* real name. Anyway, it doesn't matter, but it was a bit of luck you giving him a Tarot reading... nice of the old boy to offer to dispose of all the superfluous *belongings* in exchange wasn't it? What a great help to us all.'
Minerva shuddered and looked at David, 'Well, here we go again...'

'What do you mean?' said David, 'She doesn't have all those bags this time does she? And where is she going anyway?'
Minerva was shuffling the Tarot again, 'Well, let's face it, these

residential packages take time to sort out – it took ages with Prickly Hall I seem to remember.'

'She'll need somewhere in the interim then,' David watched the card as Minerva turned it over.

'And you know what that means don't you?'

'I think I do,' David stared at the wicked grin of the Devil. 'At least he's smiling.'

'Oh yes,' said Minerva, 'He gets away with murder you know.'

'Not here, I hope?' said David raising his eyebrows.

Minerva sighed and pulled one more card, perhaps it wouldn't be quite as bad as she thought... The Grim Reaper stared back at her from a blood spattered field of golden corn. 'With death on the cards, I'm not sure I can answer that,' she pulled the edges of her shawl closer as a cold rush of air swept across the room.

'I'm not sure I want you to,' said David, straightening his dog collar. 'Some things are better left unsaid.'

* * *

Isis hummed in absent-minded fashion as she applied her new lipstick. Pelican Pink seemed to match her pale complexion and the bright yellows and greens of her dress in a way she would never have imagined before. Thanks to Minerva's guidance and the odd dose of magic her old self had slipped behind her into the murky shadows of the past.

She was enjoying this new found freedom, unrestricted by the drab greys, browns and navy blues of old. She felt like a new woman in these post-Derek days of rainbows and pastels, in fact there wasn't a colour she wouldn't wear at all now. She still hadn't quite got the knack of mixing and matching but practise was the order of the day and no longer did she resemble a liquorice allsort (as Minerva said) but maybe closer to a rhubarb and custard... Surely two colours were better than five?

Yes, thanks to Minerva she was getting the hang of it. As well as the belly dancing classes, they'd added creative art classes to their social calendar and Isis was thoroughly enjoying her personal reinvention in ways she'd never allowed herself to imagine before. There was no doubt about it, she was flowering at last or '*coming into bloom*,' as David so very kindly put it only the other day... But then, he *was* a man of God and it was the church fete she was helping out at. However, not everyone was dressed like Isis on the day. The lilac and orange mohair twin-set with peppermint corduroy pencil skirt and salmon pink espadrilles did seem to draw a certain amount of attention. She'd never had so many people tell her how bright and cheerful she looked.

She puckered her lips in the mirror as the doorbell went and before she could answer it, Minerva flew into the hallway, hair flying behind her.

'Whatever's the matter?' said Isis, checking the front door latch, 'Are we still going to the class?'

'What?' said Minerva stopping at the mirror, 'Of course we are Isis, wouldn't miss it for the world. Life art in Cordelia Nightshade's back garden in the merry month of May with Beltane upon us?! But so is something else I must tell you about first...'

'Oh...' Isis tried her most sobering tone, 'And what is upon us, or upon *you* as well as Beltane, then?'

'In a nutshell, my mother,' Minerva dragged her fingers slowly through her fiery mane and stared hard at Isis, 'My mother has been, or rather *is being* kicked out of the home we fought so hard to get her into. Can you believe that?'

'You mean Prickly Hall...can they do that?' said Isis wondering if a pre-class tipple might be a good idea.

'They've done it, Isis. Or rather they *are* doing it. That awful prickly manager woman called yesterday to give me the news... A particularly charming delivery, laced with seething sarcasm and contempt with no sympathy whatsoever for the poor bugger who will have to take over the care of the dragon!'

Isis disappeared briefly and returned with two glasses and a small bottle of unopened brandy.

'And who will that be?' she said, passing a full glass to Minerva, 'Where will she go now?'

There was a quiet moment as Minerva took a large gulp of her drink while Isis looked at the floor.

'Where do you think?' said Minerva, 'You're looking at Crafty Care Services in case you couldn't tell.'

'But why can't she go into another home?'

'Oh believe me she will be!' snorted Minerva, 'But you know how long it took me to get her into that one... and she'll have to come and live with us first because they won't re-locate her. As far as they're concerned, if she has family, then she has somewhere to go!'

'Oh Minerva, how will you cope? It nearly drove you over the edge last time!'

'I will cope somehow, Isis.' Minerva poured herself another drink, 'I'll have to won't I? It's come as a bit of a shock, that's all. And with Morrigan around I just don't know how it's going to work,' she sighed. 'What would you do?'

Isis was taken aback. Minerva had never asked for her advice before.

'Look Minerva, it won't be forever, maybe try not to think about it too much beforehand – it'll only make things worse.'

'Worse? How could anything be worse than having my mother living with me in *my* home?'

'Well that's exactly it,' Isis was trying her best, 'but the more you think about it and talk about it, the worse it'll seem. And you won't really know until it happens will you? You always say to me that you empower something more by talking about it...and the thinking can take up more energy than the doing of it!'

Minerva stared at Isis through her glass, 'Isis, I do believe that makes quite a bit of sense. I'm impressed. But whether or not I can put those words of wisdom into practice remains to be seen.' She held her hand up to Isis, 'I know, I know. Not very positive but... what was that inscription at the door of the temple of Delphi? *Know Thyself.* And therein lies the problem.'

'I think you're looking for one Minerva.'

'I don't have to Isis, because it's here,' she pointed to herself, 'I know myself too well and I know my mother too. It will be hell on earth for both of us and anyone else in the vicinity.'

'Well maybe it's time to change then Minerva. You told me that. You said we can change ourselves *if we want to.* So isn't that the thing here? Not that you can't change, but do you really want to?'

Minerva caressed her glass slowly, turning it round and round. 'Isis,' she said in a serious manner, 'I do believe you're learning. If that's not the Goddess talking I don't know what is...'

'Good teaching you see!' laughed Isis, looking at the clock, 'Now... don't we have a naked body to look at?'

'Good lord and lady,' said Minerva, 'I think we do....and

before I forget, take this...'
She handed a small, red velvet pouch to her friend. Isis knew at once what it was. Minerva's magic was always made and packaged by her very own hands. The jagged ends of the cloth poking up were sharply tied together with a bright green ribbon.

'The colours of Beltane! How lovely, thank you!' said Isis, stroking the pouch.

'Yes of course,' said Minerva in a business-like voice, 'I took matters into my own hands and did a bit of work for you in the romance department. Not out of place I don't think, do you?'
She looked at the red faced Isis.

'Very kind of you Minerva. Can I look inside?'

'Don't be so polite, Isis, and carry it with you for a while or at least throughout Beltane. Allow it to permeate into every cell of your being and you'll be surprised what happens...'

'Will I?' Isis continued to stroke the red velvet with a look of bewilderment.

'The minute you doubt magic, stops it from happening. I've told you before Isis, believing is receiving.'

Minerva had a way with words, they seemed to conjour up something as she was speaking and charge the air with electricity. Isis couldn't explain it but knew by the butterfly in her stomach, that it excited her.

And that was enough.

She untied the tight little bundle and breathed in the earthiness of a heavy scent she didn't recognize.

'It's patchouli,' Minerva watched her closely, 'Very good for romance...has particular drawing qualities although not quite as strong as the Follow Me Boy oil – I thought it best to keep it slightly diluted in that respect. And the stone is a garnet, Spessartine to be precise, an extremely powerful stone of attraction if ever there was one. Go easy with it.'

'What do you mean?' said Isis, turning over the orange crystal in her hand and holding it up to the light. 'It's a stunning piece though, quite beautiful.'

'Just be careful in what company you are in when you carry it that's all,' said Minerva, 'It can be very magnetic. But certainly nothing to fret over Isis...it will do the job!'

Isis looked searchingly at her friend, 'I'm touched, really I am Minerva, thank you,' she said, crossing her feet as discreetly as she could.

4

The God and the Canary

Cordelia Nightshade's garden was a pleasant enough place to spend an afternoon. She may not have been the most pleasant host but Minerva thought it was a small price to pay for a spot of light entertainment. Given her circumstances the life art class appealed in more ways than one and who could blame her? The dark cloud of her mother's impending re-installment into Crafty Cottage needed lifting and she could think of nothing lighter than a man with no clothes on. The thought of it brought a smile to her face which up until now, only the brandy could give her.

With smirks on their faces, the two friends headed across the village one very warm afternoon in May.

'Isis, did you bring the brandy by any chance?' said Minerva, feeling around in her bag.

'No, afraid not,' said Isis, 'Won't Cordelia have anything?'

'Not sure it's that sort of affair,' said Minerva, 'But one never knows, Cruella de Ville has been known to splash out on the odd occasion, it would certainly make a change from the cucumber and salmon sarnies' she usually comes up with and that awful Lapsang tea that tastes of burning embers.'

'Remember, this is only the second time I've met the woman,' said Isis, 'And after that first class you took me to, I don't remember much apart from feeling quite faint when she removed the sheet from that statue...'

Minerva laughed, 'Oh yes, you do struggle with nudity don't you?'

'Not as much as I used to Minerva. My shrinking violet days are a thing of the past, at least I hope they are anyway,' said Isis gathering speed. 'Can we not talk about it please!'

'No, you're absolutely right, the last thing we want is you getting all prudish and silly over a piece of life art with no clothes on. Let's put it out of our minds before it becomes an issue shall we?'

'Well, you brought it up. I wish I'd brought the brandy now.'

'Shall we make a quick detour to the village shop?' said Minerva looking behind her, 'It'll only take us five minutes...'

'No Minerva! Can we please just keep going and if you talk nicely to Cruella...'

'*Cordelia,* Isis, for Goddess sake don't come out with that otherwise we'll be out on our ear. She can be the most formidable tyrant at times, you know. But she does bear an uncanny resemblance to the Dalmation woman doesn't she? She even talks like her!'

'Oh dear,' said Isis wringing her hands, 'I feel a bit peculiar!'

Minerva came to an abrupt halt and planted both hands on the bird-like shoulders, looking straight at her, 'Isis,' she said firmly, 'Calm down! Lots of deep breaths and wipe from your mind all images of naked people and that devil of a woman. Replace with large jugs of iced Pimms and many bottles of wine and with a bit of luck, that's what we'll get...it's easy when you know how. Visualization is the keystone to magic, I'm telling you.'

Isis was trying her hardest, 'Yes, you keep telling me Minerva.' She wriggled free and continued to walk with quiet determination - a fluttering of yellow and green chiffon sticking in damp patches to the small of her back. She reminded Minerva of a canary escaped from its cage, unsure and frightened of its own freedom.

'Do you have your pouch on you? said Minerva.

Isis clasped at her chest, 'Yes, I put it where you said…although why here and now I shall never know!'

Minerva winked and a wicked grin crept over her face which only served to unnerve Isis even more. In no time at all, they had reached their destination and after the polite formalities on arrival were directed to the garden by an orange skinned Cordelia Nightshade in a pink toga. 'Do make your way round the back ladies and help yourself to a drink on the way. Pimms on the side and wine in the fridge! Excuse me while I see to our model for today…' Her voice trailed off as she slithered down the hallway, in the direction of the garden.

Minerva led the way into the kitchen and turned to a startled faced Isis, 'Now, what are we having?' she said picking two glasses and holding them aloft, 'Will it be Pimms or wine?'

'I don't know how you do it Minerva. It's —'

'—like magic?'

'Well yes, I can't think of anything else to describe it,' said a bewildered looking Isis.

'I find it best not to question it,' said Minerva, filling a tall glass with Pimms and fishing out the strawberries and cucumbers. 'And it looks like there's plenty more where this came from … But now for the in-flight entertainment.'

She gestured to the garden where the rest of the class were assembled.

Isis looked at the bobbing heads and waving clipboards, thinking how much they reminded her of her uncle Dylan's chickens from her childhood days. They were huddled around a bright pink chaise lounge, their squawking punctuated by the occasional outburst of laughter. Isis had no idea what they were talking about but it made her feel edgy.

'Come on Isis, we don't want to miss the show do we?'

Isis followed Minerva into the garden to join the hen party, heart thudding against her ribcage. She felt someone brush past her on the way and caught a flash of tanned male body with only a bright pink towel to cover his modesty. A strong whiff of Old Spice trailed behind him when he swaggered past and all the heads turned as he sat down ceremoniously on the chaise lounge in silence, staring into the distance.

For a split second Isis met his gaze and a small electric shock rippled through her body. The Nightshade woman stepped towards him and she saw him nod while his hand felt for the towel. He looked like a God.

The hen party and Cruella moved closer still and something snapped in Isis. She couldn't bear it any longer… 'Please!' she wailed, 'You don't have to… really you don't!'

Jumping in front of the stunned God, she turned to the sea of gawping faces, 'Surely he needn't go the whole way? I mean, it's not absolutely necessary is it?'

She seemed to plead with every fragile bone in her body, which was far from pitiful. In fact it was a genuinely courageous act prompting an earthy grin from the God and a look of plain horror from the deadly nightshade woman.

'For heaven's sake!' snorted Cordelia, moving in on the

intruder, 'This is a life art class and all perfectly in keeping with the usual proceedings. What *is* your problem?'

The God shifted uneasily on the chaise lounge and fought back a smile. He thought how like a canary the yellow and green wisp of a woman looked compared to the vulture -like Cordelia.

'I don't have a problem r-really,' stuttered the canary, 'It's just that, well, I'm new to this sort of thing and...'

'No,' rumbled the fearsome vulture, narrowing her eyes at Isis, 'I didn't think we'd seen you before. Who did you come with?'

At that point, a flaming head of red hair appeared from the back of the group and joined them. 'Calm down Cordelia. My friend means well, surely you can see that!'

'Minerva...I might have known. How very *typical!*' she looked sideways at Isis, 'Yes, I seem to recall you mentioning your *new friend* at the last meeting although I'm not sure she is entirely suited to a life art group, wouldn't you agree?'

'Now then, Cordelia, there's no need for that,' said Minerva, 'This class has always been inclusive in every way, surely we can sort this out without things getting out of hand...keep your hair on!'

The God smirked in an un-godly manner while the small canary fluttered about in front of him. He didn't have the foggiest what was going on but had a distinct feeling the host had met her match in the fiery red head – possibly some unfinished business playing out - and was pleased to see some justice for the tiny bird who was easy meat for a vulture like Miss Nightshade; a deadly woman if ever he'd met one. Feeling a certain sense of responsibility towards the smaller bird and leaving the two bigger ones to battle it out, he rearranged his pink loin cloth and gently manoeuvred Isis to one side.

'Are you alright?' he murmured.

'I'm fine, thank you,' she whispered.

'I'm glad to hear it, but not convinced I'm afraid...Would you like a glass of water or something stronger perhaps?'

He made a conscious effort to maintain eye contact with her, it was the least he could do. The poor thing was shaking and her wobbling pile of coppery hair was familiar to him, but he couldn't think why.

She placed a fragile hand on his shoulder to steady herself. 'I'd like that, yes please. I'm so sorry for upsetting things. I don't quite know what came over me,' she sighed. 'I'm not normally prudish or anything but there was something in that woman's eyes...' She glanced nervously at the deadly Nightshade woman and back at him again, 'It was ugly and you looked so *unspoilt* I suppose, that I had this urge to do something...so I did.'

The God laughed, 'You certainly did! And to be honest, I'm glad you did.'

'Are you?'

'Don't sound so surprised,' he said holding out his hand, 'I'm Gerald, by the way...'

'Oh...' she said, 'I'm Isis.'

'Isis.' The name lingered on his lips as a dreamy expression crept over his face.

She laughed and stared back. It was one of those moments when there is nothing else to say, but the silence wasn't uncomfortable. In fact Isis was surprised how easy she found his company.

They fell into perfect step beside each other and she beamed at him.

'Ribena,' said Isis, 'There's a big jug of it inside... shall we grab a glass?'

'Now you're talking,' said Gerald, 'Any ginger biscuits?'

'How did you know that?' she said, straightening her hairpiece.

'Oh I have a feeling for these things,' he winked at her.

'Psychic are you?'

'That's one way of putting it,' he stopped, 'Let's just say I take after my grandmother who was a very *magical* lady.'

'Oh I see,' smiled Isis, 'I'm quite used to Witches if that's what you mean... I have one as a friend.'

'Would you like another?' said Gerald, 'Men can be Witches too.'

'Oh.' Isis looked at him, 'You do seem to have appeared quite like magic, I mean you know, sort of out of the blue...'

'It's how it works,' he said, 'But actually, it's the most natural thing in the world.'

'That's just what Minerva says!'

'Is this your friend, the Witch?'

She let out a soft gasp as her hand flew to her chest, 'It must've worked' she said almost to herself.

He laughed, 'Ah, been stirring the cauldron have we?'

He knew. Isis felt her cheeks burning and a fluttering in her stomach. Minerva could read her like a book and now here was the male equivalent right beside her, showing an interest *in her.* Could she handle it? She looked at his golden skin and the sparkle in those eyes and wondered no more. 'To answer your question,' she said, ignoring his last remark, 'I think I'd like that...another friend sounds lovely.'

She couldn't quite work out where the nerve had come from, but it was her voice and they were her words.

'I'm very glad you said that.'

Isis clutched her stomach as the fluttering got worse.

'Are you okay?' said Gerald.

'Yes...yes I'm fine,' said Isis, 'I just get a bit...'

A warm hand touched her shoulder and she felt instantly calm.

'There's nothing to worry about,' he said with a firm squeeze, 'Nothing at all.'

'Thank you,' said Isis, 'I'm very glad you said that.'

Laughter is a funny thing. It flows backwards and forwards like a magical current between people, charging every atom with its power. Up until then, Isis thought it was only angels who walked on air. But right now, for once, she was quite happy to be wrong.

5

The Last Supper

Minerva paced up and down the kitchen as a plume of smoke from the cooker swirled around her. When she was feeling unsettled like this she sought comfort in two things: brandy and the company of those she loved. And so, indulging in large amounts of her favourite tipple she prepared for the arrival of her nearest and dearest.

They were all coming to dinner. She wondered where David was…it was his idea. She was almost certain he'd offered to cook and was absolutely certain she would have agreed. Minerva's culinary skills left much to be desired. Cooking was something she did because she had to but rarely enjoyed, the only exception being when she was looking after her granddaughter. She took great pleasure in the simplicity of chopping up apples and making the 'eggy soldiers' which Morrigan loved. Who wouldn't delight in the joys of baking with a two year old? A messy kitchen had a dramatic effect on the psyche and creating out of chaos was the kind of spontaneous magic she enjoyed making.

The doorbell interrupted her ponderings and before she

knew it, David was there in front of her glowing like an angel.

'Sorry I'm late, had a bit of church business to attend to,' he looked past her and grimaced at the smoke before kissing her softly on the lips, 'I'll take over shall I?'

'It's all yours chef,' Minerva purred, 'And so am I.'

David laughed while placing his jacket on the hat stand and proceeded to open a window and let the smoke out.

'What time is everyone coming?' he said scanning the room.

'About eight-ish I think,' said Minerva, 'Can't have a Last Supper starting too early can we?'

David looked at her, 'Last Supper..?'

'You know what I mean David,' said Minerva, handing him a bottle of beer and pouring herself a brandy, 'Before a certain person arrives next week.'

'Ah, your mother!'

He never drinks from the bottle, thought Minerva.

'Quite,' she said, 'If ever there was a reasonable and valid excuse for my madness, she is it. I'm dreading it David, have you any words of heavenly wisdom? Because by the Goddess, I need it now more than ever!'

'It won't be forever Minerva.'

She could hardly hear him, 'No, but it will feel like it and that's *far* worse. Have you any idea what I am about to endure and more to the point, will you help me bear this heavy cross?'

'Minerva, there's no need...'

'There is *every* need,' said Minerva through clenched teeth.

David hadn't seen her this mad since they'd moved her mother out of her house with all the bags. The Squalor Skips episode was deeply ingrained in his memory, a painful reminder of Minerva's unpredictable and volcanic relationship with her mother. He'd played an admirable supporting role, but most of the time found it best to stand well back while the fireworks went off in all directions.

'Sometimes it helps if you can see the barriers…,' said David quietly, 'as only obstacles to overcome...'

'David,' she was talking under her breath now, 'The only thing I can see at the moment is my mother living in this house, *my* house. Overcoming that is a mountain I just can't face…'

With that, she burst into tears and David held her firm against him where they remained locked like puzzle pieces until the doorbell heralded the first guests.

* * *

Joe didn't have a watch. He'd never needed one - having always relied on the sun's position for telling the time - and working so close with the outside elements he found it the most natural form of time keeping.

He was pretty sure Ronnie had said about eight. The lights were on and he could smell something cooking but he must have been standing on the Crafty doorstep for at least five minutes and no-one had answered. After ringing her mobile number he was relieved when she picked up almost straight away.

'Ron are you in? At the cottage I mean?'

'Yes, of course I am. Where else would I be? Where are you?'

'Outside on the doorstep, but no-one's answering...'

'Well Mum *is* there - I heard her in the kitchen earlier - and David's there too. I could've sworn the doorbell went about half an hour ago.'

'What are you doing? Come and let us in will you?'

'*Trying* to get Morrigan off to sleep is what I'm *doing*. You know how tricky she can be, especially when she hears voices and things going on!'

'Well there's nothing going on at the moment Ron, apart from me standing on the doorstep like an idiot!'

'Okay, give me a minute...'

A quick peep at the sleeping child in her cot and the mirror on the way out was enough to reassure Ronnie that both Morrigan and her appearance were doing what they were meant to. Papa Joe the bear and the tiny child were locked in a tight embrace, the only movement was the rise and fall of her chest. Another peek into the empty kitchen on the way to the front door revealed the carnage typical of her mother's culinary skills. But no Minerva.

Joe grinned and kissed her frown away as she opened the door.

'No idea where Mum is,' said Ronnie shaking her head without taking her eyes off him.

'She *must* be here, surely,' said Joe, peering into the kitchen at the mess. They ventured through the hall and into a living room of flickering candle light.

Ronnie called out as quietly as she could across the room, 'Mum!'

Just visible in the half-light, David and Minerva were cuddled up on the sofa in silence.

'Hey you two,' said Joe softly, 'Everything okay?'

The figures slowly peeled away from each other.

'Yes, thank you,' said David clearing his throat, 'Just a quiet moment needed that's all.'

'What's the matter Mum?' said Ronnie.

'I'm fine now darling,' said a sleepy Minerva, 'Just one of my funny turns that's all. Thank the Goddess for David is all I can say.'

David rose from the comfort of the sofa, 'I'll get on with the dinner. You stay here Minerva and relax.'

He bent to plant a kiss on the top of her head and got a mouthful of thick red hair in the process. Minerva managed a weak smile, 'You're a wonder, really you are,' she sighed before slumping back onto the sofa.

Ronnie disappeared and returned with a full glass of brandy and handed it to her mother, 'Here we are Mum, something to get you back on track...'

'Thank you darling.'

'Anything you want to talk about?'

Minerva sat up and inhaled deeply, 'If I have to…it's your grandmother.'

'Is she all right? What's happened?'

'Oh she's more than all right,' Minerva turned the glass around in her hands, 'Up to her usual tricks according to the manager of Prickly Hall.'

'Nothing new there then,' laughed Ronnie, 'Doing what she does best...giving them all a run for their money!'

Minerva took a large slug of her drink, 'Not for much longer Ron...'

'What do you mean?'

'In a nutshell, they're kicking her out.'

'So where's she going?' Ronnie looked hard at her mother, 'Don't tell me...'

Minerva raised both eyebrows and touched Ronnie's hand, 'Hopefully it won't be for long darling. I'm sure we'll manage.'

Ronnie pulled her hand away slowly, 'But I won't be here Mum. Joe and I are going to live together,' the words toppled out, 'Ropey left his boat to Joe and we're going to live on it. A great opportunity don't you think?'

Minerva stared at her drink, 'Oh well, that *is* good news Ron...for you all, really it is. I'm pleased for you. Yes, I'm sure I'll manage fine with your grandmother...you know me. I love a challenge!'

She forced herself to smile just as the doorbell went. David poked his head round the living room door, 'Isis and Gerald are here.' He shot her a questioning look of concern to which she responded by springing up from the sofa. Ronnie was not fooled, she knew her mother too well.

'Mum, we'll talk about it tomorrow yes?'

'Ron there's nothing else to talk about. You've got Joe and Morrigan and that's wonderful. I've got David and my mother. Quite a contrast isn't it? Heaven and hell if you please! But then I never do anything by halves do I? My life is a constant flow of undulations, from one extreme to another. The eternal battle between the darkness and the light is what magic is all about Ronnie. And if ever I forget that minor detail, the universe always finds a way to remind me!'

'I'm glad you see it that way Mum,' said Ronnie.

'It's the *only* way to see it,' said Minerva on her way to the door, 'Now, enough of all that and let's see our guests in shall we? Can you put some music on Ron? Something romantic I think...it's early days for Isis and Gerald and I do like to help create the right *ambience*.'

Ronnie was grateful for the new arrivals, it was amazing how people could change the environment just by being there - and Isis with a man, now *that* was going to be interesting. She flicked through her mother's album collection and found Angel Wings on Strings by the Halo Quartet. She'd never heard of them before but it sounded ideal and hopefully would help the night go with a swing. She giggled to herself at the thought of it, although she was sure her mother would more than contribute in that department.

Minerva was quite the hostess when she wanted to be.

* * *

The night certainly did go with a swing. David managed to reverse the chaos in the kitchen, salvage what was left and produce a delicious meal for everyone. Minerva managed to drink a lot more brandy and charm Gerald and Joe without causing too much embarrassment for Isis, who was looking slightly less anxious than usual.

Concentrating on her guests gave Minerva a focus other than the impending doom filled thoughts of her mother coming to stay. That would happen soon enough. Until then, she was enjoying herself in the company of people she loved and living for the moment.

Armed with a stack of wobbling, empty plates, Minerva headed for the kitchen, 'Coffee anyone?' she called over her shoulder.

'Is it real?' said Gerald without so much of a twitch of an eyebrow.

Isis began to fiddle with her serviette.

'I'll see what I can do,' she replied, 'Pardon me while I go and pick and grind a bean or two. I suppose you take cream with that as well?'

'How did you guess Minerva?' said Gerald, 'Very astute.'

Minerva couldn't resist poking her head around the door, 'One doesn't have to be psychic to pick up on a basic human need, wouldn't you agree?'

Gerald laughed, 'Most definitely. Couldn't start or finish my day without it...'

'Really?' said Isis, 'You have it before bed? Doesn't it keep you awake?'

'Indeed it does,' said Gerald with a grin.

The silence was palpable as awkward glances flitted across the table in the direction of a very red Isis.

'I'm a hot chocolate man myself,' said Joe, giving Isis one of his beaming smiles, 'With marshmallows and sprinkles...goes down a treat before putting the guitar to bed for the night!' he winked at Ronnie.

'Did you bring it Joe?' said David, 'A few tunes would be the perfect end to a lovely evening. If not, there's mine over there.' He pointed to a guitar standing in the corner under Minerva's beloved Green Man painting.

'I haven't got it with me, no, but if you don't mind?'

'Feel free, please,' said David, 'I'm always pleased to hear it played and especially by a musician far better than myself.'

Joe laughed as he picked up the guitar, 'Flattery from a vicar...now that can't be bad!'

He played and they listened and Minerva thought how it was the perfect ending to a night in spite of how it had started. It was at that moment, her mother crept back into her thoughts.

'Are you all right Minerva?' David leaned in close to her as the music rippled around the room.

He seemed to have a knack for tuning into her instantly.

'Yes, I think so,' she said with slight hesitation, 'Oh, just one of those black clouds looming if you must know.'

'I don't suppose it has your mother sitting on it?'

'You could say that,' said Minerva, 'Although I can tell you for certain she was not playing a bloody harp!'

'Now why doesn't that surprise me?' David laughed, 'Not quite ready for the celestial spheres yet is she?'

'No. Not ever,' said Minerva, 'And I'm not sure she'd even get into hell, even *that's* too nice a place for someone like her.'

'Ah,' said David, 'Must be why she's coming here then!'

Minerva dug her nails into his arm, 'I'm relying on you, David, especially now Ronnie's going....they're moving onto a boat! I will be here on my own with my mother, can you imagine it?'

He didn't answer straight away, choosing to sit there in a calm silence. It went on for longer than usual and it made her nervous.

'David, what are you thinking? Please say something, *anything* to remove this black cloud and impending feeling of doom. It's oppressive and suffocating and I can't stand it!'

David led her gently into the hallway and signalled her to sit on the stairs.

'Minerva, listen to me,' he said firmly but gently, 'You *will* cope and you will get through this next challenge, and it may feel like your toughest one yet, but you have absolutely what it takes to face it. Why? Because, firstly: you are made of stronger stuff than you realize - all you need to do is believe it - and secondly: this is your mother we are talking about here. And whatever your reasons may be for the way you feel - and I don't doubt they are valid – it will not do you any good dwelling on them.

This is your chance to let go of the past, make your peace with it *and* your mother. I've told you before, remember when Ronnie came home from the hospital with Morrigan? You were terrified how you were going to cope! But you did.

You coped then and you will again this time, and I'll support you - that's a given - but ultimately it will come from you. The human spirit is stronger than we think, divine in essence. And yours is no less than and all the more magical *because* of it. Every challenge is an opportunity to grow and become stronger and you can do it. I know you can.'

He sat down on the stairs and resting both elbows on his knees, continued to focus his whole attention on her, 'Still there?'

She gave him a puzzled look.

'I'm talking about that black cloud. I don't see one,' said David looking above her head.

'Don't you?' she whispered back, 'I'm glad about that. Thank you for lifting it although you may have started a drop of rain in the process...'

She wiped away hot tears with the back of her hand, 'You're a magician, there's no doubt about it. I feel very different, much better...thank you.'

'Always a pleasure,' said David taking her hand and squeezing it, 'Anything for you...you know that!'

'I do now,' said Minerva, 'Are you sure you're not really Merlin beneath that vicarly exterior?'

David shot her a wicked gleam, 'I would have thought you of all people would be best qualified to answer that question Minerva.'

'How good of you to remind me.' Minerva glanced at the living room door, 'Shall we round up the stragglers and retreat to the bedroom for further enquiries?'

6

Hagstones and Millponds

The old woman narrowed her eyes at the soft rapping on the door and cocked her white head of hair to one side. The door opened slowly to reveal a small round figure carrying a tray.

'Morning Cybele,' said the figure, 'breakfast is served!'

The voice was far too cheerful.

'I don't want any bloody breakfast,' growled the old woman. 'And who are you anyway? You're not one of the usual lot.'

The figure moved into focus, approaching the bed where the old woman lay awkwardly in a semi-horizontal position. With one hand she began to collect the half-eaten biscuits and crumpled balls of tissue from the bedside table and placed a mug of pale brown liquid in their place.

'Yes, I am one of the usual staff. You know me Cybele,' she said. 'It's Brigid. I've been here quite a while now.'

'Who's frigid?' the old woman shouted, 'Don't know you from Adam. Go on, piss off!'

'After you've had some of this, Cybele,' said an unruffled Brigid, placing a bowl next to the mug and stuffing the tissues in her pocket.

'What's that?' The old woman pointed at the bulge in the blue and white checked tunic, 'You've stolen something! You're always taking something, you lot. Bunch of bloody thieves, the lot of you!'

Brigid sighed and glanced quickly at the watch pinned to her large bosom, 'Cybele, are you going to eat your porridge before it gets cold?'

The old woman was shuffling out of the ruffled sheets and reaching for the metal frame propped close by. 'I need the loo,' she grunted, before pulling herself up in a series of jerks onto the frame. 'Don't you nick anything else while I'm gone, I know what you're like - all the same you lot. Nothing changes in this place. Hell on earth, that's what it is!'

The mumbling continued as she slowly made her way to the bathroom, only a few feet from her bed.

'I won't touch a thing Cybele, never you mind about that,' said Brigid, looking at her watch again. 'Can you manage in there?'

The clunking sounds of the frame moving across the floor coupled with the grunting from the old woman were familiar to Brigid. She'd become used to the ways of old people in the six short months working as a carer at Prickly Hall. However, this one was quite a challenge because there was a certain feistiness about Cybele Crafty - if the rude and obnoxious exterior could be overlooked, which Brigid's good nature allowed - and beneath it was a courageous spirit which was hard not to admire.

At a guess, Brigid imagined she'd had a hard life. There was always a good reason behind bad behaviour and believing the best about people had helped her cope with the trials of working in a care home. It wasn't an easy job and not everyone could do it, but Brigid was doing all right so far. She tried not to listen too much to the other members of staff – they could be a whiney bunch – preferring instead to get on with her work.

It was good to be busy, it took the mind off things.

'Are you all right in there Cybele?' she called to the half shut door, 'Do you need a hand?'

'Where's the bog roll? I can't see it.'

Brigid finished straightening out the sheets on the bed and joined the old woman.

'Here we are Cybele,' she handed a brand new roll to the hunched figure on the toilet, 'It was right under your nose.'

'How would I know you silly bitch?' said Cybele, 'You know I'm nearly blind and none of you care! You'd just leave me here...and then rifle through my drawers. You think I'm bloody daft! I know what you're all up to!'

'That's not true and you know it,' Brigid almost sang the words as she proceeded to clean up after the old woman as she dropped the half scrunched up paper onto the floor. 'Let's go and get you dressed and then you can have your porridge before it gets cold.'

'Has it got prunes?' she squawked, 'I always have prunes, they help me go!'

The old woman and her frame shuffled out.

'You've just *been,* Cybele,' said Brigid following her out.

'Have I?'

Holding her nose without physically pinching her nostrils was a well practiced skill Brigid had picked up from those nappy changing days of early motherhood. She was glad of it now, especially.

While Cybele gobbled her porridge Brigid busied herself with more tidying up and began to take clothes out of the drawers, placing them into neat piles on the dressing table.

'What are you doing you silly bitch?' said the old woman, wiping her mouth and throwing the tissue aside.

'Don't you remember Cybele? It's Friday today and someone special is coming to take you out, for the weekend. It'll make a nice change won't it?'

Brigid carried on with the clothes, carefully removing the piles and putting them into a large holdall.

'What do you mean taking me out? I don't want to go out. I never go out. You'll take all my things.' Globules of the sticky porridge dribbled from the old woman's mouth, 'That's why you've arranged it. Bloody tea-leaf!'

Brigid ducked just in time as the spoon flew past her and hit the mirror of the dressing table and caught her own tired reflection as the clumps stuck like glue to the shiny surface.

'Cybele,' she said, 'Your daughter will be here soon to pick you up. Shall we sort out what you're going to wear? The blue or the black and white dress?'

'I haven't got any clothes...they're all gone!' said the old woman spitting out her false teeth and belching loudly, 'And why is my daughter coming? She never comes to see me. That's another stupid bitch!'

'She came the other day to see you,' said Brigid, 'And she's coming shortly... Won't it be lovely to go and stay with her for the weekend?'

'Lovely, my arse!' spat the old woman, 'You're all the bloody same.'

Your daughter isn't, thought Brigid. No, she's quite different.

* * *

Strolling along with a sleeping toddler was the perfect opportunity for a spot of daydreaming for Ronnie. She had a lot to get her head round and there was nothing like being out in the fresh air for getting things into perspective.

As she ambled through the narrow country lanes and back through the village she could literally feel the tension draining from her body and her head beginning to clear. By the time the village shop came into view, thoughts of chocolate slowed her down to a final halt outside. She could do with the sugar.

'Lovely to see you again Ron, it's been far too long,' said the smartly dressed young woman peering under the hood of the buggy, 'Does she always sleep so soundly?'

'Sophia! smiled Ronnie, 'When she's tired, yes. And she's had a couple of broken nights lately. I think she picks up on things you know?'

'What kind of *things*?'

'Oh, atmospheres and people's feelings...'

'You mean in a psychic way,' said the young woman, leaning back against a green car door.

'Well yeah, but it's quite natural isn't it?' said Ronnie.

'It's probably more natural in your family than most, Ron! What's been going on?'

Ronnie glanced quickly across at the Old Druid and back at her friend, 'It's great to see you Sophia...but you wouldn't believe me if I told you.'

'Try me. Fancy a quick half outside?' Sophia nodded toward the pub, 'I've got time for a catch up if you have!'

Ronnie checked the sleeping child and glanced across at the pub, 'Yeah, why not eh? I was just killing a bit of time anyway.

It's all very *tense* at home at the moment. It's really good to see you Sophia.'

The two young women picked up an easy stride together, Sophia linking her arm through Ronnie's and dropping the car keys into her bag. They crossed the road, entering the back of the Old Druid into a small garden alive with white blossom and made their way over to a wooden table almost hidden under the snowy boughs of a huge cherry tree.

'What are you having?' asked Sophia, heading for the back entrance, 'The usual?'

Ronnie grinned as she steered the buggy beneath the branches of the old tree, 'Oh go on then, you've twisted my arm, I haven't had a decent drop of Druid fluid for ages!'

It was good to see Sophia. Not that she'd been avoiding her, not on a conscious level, but perhaps she'd pushed their friendship to the back of her mind, where all the painful memories were. Where Bob was filed away.

She'd had some great times with Sophia at the livery yard, they'd become good friends just like their horses. But as the memories came back she braced herself and stared hard at the blossom. She knew that everything moved in cycles – it was one of her mother's mantras - but what happened when that natural cycle was broken with an accident, what then? How did anyone get their head around losing loved ones before their time?

Yes, Ropey had just died, but he was old. Of course it was sad but he'd lived a long life and it was kind of expected and easier to accept.

Accidents were different. They ripped lives apart in a flash. What kind of a cycle was that? A broken one as far as Ronnie could see.

Sophia returned with drinks and a beaming smile, 'You look miles away Ron!'

'Cheers,' said Ronnie taking her cider, 'Yeah well, just thinking about stuff. You know, down the yard and all that. We had such good times didn't we? Feels like a lifetime away now.'

Sophia smiled and pointed at the buggy, 'Your daughter's lifetime to be precise.'

Ronnie nodded and bit her lip, 'Tell me your news, what have you been up to? Still got Kismet? Is there a *man* in the equation yet and if not, why not?'

They both laughed and stopped as Morrigan's eyelids began to flutter.

'I don't want to break the spell,' whispered Sophia, 'She looks positively angelic.'

'Oh that's because she is, when she's sleeping,' Ronnie spoke into the bottom of her glass before taking a long swig, 'You haven't answered my question. Come on, before she wakes up!'

'Right, okay,' Sophia hesitated, 'Well yes, I still have Kismet but I have to confess to not riding her as much anymore - not since...'

'I knew it! Who is he?'

Sophia shuffled awkwardly and hesitated, 'Well, to be honest with you, it's not a *he*.'

Ronnie drew back and opened her mouth to speak but nothing came out.

'That's it, you've got it,' said Sophia holding her gaze with big eyes, 'It's a she. I have a girlfriend. We met at Uni.'

'Oh. So is *she* studying to be a lawyer too?'

'No. Diana's studying to be a vet, which is quite handy,'

grinned Sophia, stretching herself up to full height, 'There, I've said it. Now you know. So.....does it surprise you?'

Ronnie put her drink down and thought for a moment, 'Well yes, yes of course it does if I'm honest Sophia. But I tell you what,' she grimaced as both eyebrows shot up to meet her dark brown fringe, 'You could've fooled me. I had no idea - I thought you were into blokes is what I'm trying to say!'

Sophia laughed, 'Well I am! I mean I *was*. But then Diana came along and everything changed. I didn't plan it, or rather *we* didn't plan it.'

'No,' said Ronnie, 'You can't plan stuff like that can you? It just sort of happens I suppose, doesn't it?'

'Exactly, yes. She's a really nice person though and guess what? I'm teaching her to ride!'

Ronnie spat out a mouthful of cider as their eyes met and the friends collapsed into a fit of giggling.

The buggy began to rock as two chubby legs kicked off the blanket.

'Oh my God,' said Ronnie almost choking, 'That was priceless, you always did have a way with words!'

'Well I guess the training's paying off then,' said Sophia, dabbing her eyes with a tissue, 'Not sure how that kind of behaviour would go down in a law court but as you'd say Ron, better out than in.'

They raised their glasses and drank deeply.

'I know someone else who'd agree with that,' said Ronnie, glancing at the rocking buggy, 'Great to see you again Sophia, and for what it's worth – I couldn't give a damn if it's Arthur or Martha you're with.'

'I'm really glad you think so, Ron. I couldn't agree more.' She glanced at the buggy and quickly back at Ronnie, 'Now tell me, what's going on at home at the moment? You say things are a bit tense.'

'Oh God, yeah Mum is freaking out big time. My Gran's been kicked out of the old people's home and is coming to stay until they've sorted her out somewhere else,' Ronnie shrugged, 'You can imagine can't you?'

'I can, but I can't see your mother putting up with it...at all. But then she's got you hasn't she? So that'll help.'

'Er no it won't, because I won't be there for much longer,' said Ronnie, un-strapping the disgruntled toddler and peeling her from the buggy, 'Joe's asked me to move in with him. Me and Morrigan.'

'So you and Joe got it together then? Why am I not surprised?'

Ronnie beamed at her, 'Yeah, it was kind of on the cards for a while wasn't it? But you know what Sophia, he's brilliant with Morrigan even though she's not his and please, no more reminders of drunken stable parties...'

'Okay, I won't. Do you keep in touch with Gavin by the way? Didn't he go to Australia?'

'Yes that's right, he did. Went to shoe horses at his brother's place if you remember. And no, I don't keep in touch with him, there's no need. He doesn't know.'

'You haven't told him he has a daughter?'

'Why should I when I'm perfectly happy with Joe? He thinks the world of Morrigan and she loves him just like a dad. We're a family and I want to keep it that way, so please, no lectures. What Gavin doesn't know can't hurt him, so why spoil it?'

Sophia was quiet for a few seconds, 'Well, that's great for you all I guess, but maybe not so great for your poor mother! Where are you going to live then? Round here?'

'Yes, actually,' said Ronnie, 'Down the marina where Joe

works. Do you remember an old guy called Ropey who Joe worked with?'

'I think so, yes.'

'Well he pegged it, sadly, a few weeks ago and he left the Dutch barge he lived on, to Joe!'

'A boat,' Sophia said it slowly, 'How very cool. When?'

Ronnie pulled Morrigan into her arms, 'As soon as we can. It's empty, so it seems daft not to go for it don't you think?'

'Yes you might as well... And your grandmother? When is she arriving?'

'Oh hell,' Ronnie checked her phone, 'Today! Mum said she was picking her up sometime around now. David's going with her, which is a relief.'

'Oh that's good,' said Sophia, 'Thank God for him eh? He's quite the angelic boyfriend isn't he?'

'He certainly is,' said Ronnie in a serious voice, 'And Mum's going to need every bit of help she can get. They've never got on - her and Gran - so yeah, tension will be running high at Crafty Cottage.' She let out a heavy sigh.

'Light the blue touch paper and stand well back then?' Sophia said to Morrigan who was watching the two young women with great intensity.

'Yes, you could say that' said Ronnie, finishing the last of her drink, 'There'll be fireworks all right.'

* * *

Minerva could feel the heat rising up the back of her neck and spreading like a stain over her chest. It wasn't a good time for a hot flush. They were bad enough by themselves but add the tropical environment of an old people's home into the equation and it was like being on fire in a greenhouse.

She huffed and puffed her way through the empty corridors of Prickly Hall, home for the living dead. It's just like a ghost house but hotter, she thought, as she tried to fan the flush out of her system with a brochure she picked up from the entrance.

Where were they all? She couldn't help noticing the occasional resident hunched over themselves in the corner of their small rooms, an open door displaying them like some showpiece in a museum.

It made her feel sad. What kind of lives had they had? Every one of them was somebody's daughter or son at the very least and for most of them this was their final stopping point while they bided their time, waiting for the inevitable curtain call.

She shuddered, where was David? He said he'd meet her there. She needed him. Dealing with her mother today was not going to be easy and definitely not something she could do alone even if she wanted to. Stopping to get her bearings and collecting her wits, she tried to run hot, sweaty fingers through her hair but it was no good. The heat had made it fuzzy and the knots were worse than usual. Fumbling around in her bag for a hair-tie she noticed a charm pouch she'd made up a while ago for strength and protection. Just what she needed.

She pressed the soft velvet cloth against her hot cheeks and breathed in the heady scent. She remembered making it at the last new moon - the beginning of a new cycle – and the unmistakable sweetness of cinnamon and its rough, shards of bark poking through reminded her of the healing strength of her own spirit. She untied the drawstring and felt the protection of the bay leaves and the call of remembrance from the sprig of rosemary, all gathered from the garden. Digging deeper, she found a hagstone from one of her many beach combing trips. These were the stones of raw, earth magic and she ran her finger around it and through the hole to remember the power she had imbued it with.

There was nothing better than the bones of the earth and the plant spirits to remind her of the magic in her blood. Full of gratitude and renewed intention she resolved to focus on this energy and draw from its power whenever she needed it.

But there was one more thing in the pouch. Minerva smiled at the Oak leaf and remembered where it had come from. She had been in awe of its majesty when she'd spotted it at the vicarage, swooning like a schoolgirl, hugging its massive trunk and stroking the branches before picking as many of the fallen leaves as she could. Only Mother Nature, the Earth Goddess, could come up with a work of art like that. The spidery veins reached out to her, spreading across the paper thin surface... She felt stronger already.

'Minerva, there you are. Are you okay?'

She smiled dreamily at him.

'You've broken the spell,' she whispered as she kissed him, 'But I'm not complaining, you do have a knack for turning up at the right time.'

'Oh I'm glad you see it that way,' David grinned, 'I got caught up with the bell ringers, not literally, but it was necessary I'm afraid. There was much to discuss.' He looked at her and squeezed her arm, 'I thought you might be a bit uptight, but you look positively radiant.'

'I feel like a millpond, actually'.

'What a wonderful analogy. You haven't been on the brandy have you?'

Smiling, Minerva held up the pouch, before putting it back in her bag. 'Not a drop. Just recharging with a bit of magic.'

'Well I'm glad to see its working,' said David, 'How long will it last?'

'As long as it takes for any ripples to appear,' Minerva wiped her hair from her face, 'I'm relying on you to hold them at bay for as long as you can.'

'I'll do my best,' said David taking her hand and continuing along the corridor.

With Minerva's mother there was no telling how long that would be. 'Remember still waters run deep,' he said to her as he punched in the code to the last set of doors.

'What's that supposed to mean?'

'What it means,' said David, 'is, by keeping your mind in one place, focused on God or Goddess – whatever you want to call it - those waters will remain calm.'

'You mean the bit that loves unconditionally?'

'That's a good way of putting it Minerva,' he said, 'Think about how difficult it's going to be for your mother perhaps...'

She stopped and looked at him, 'I'm going to try, really I am David....but...'

He pressed his finger against her lips and kissed her as beads of sweat began to prick at the base of her neck and trickle down her back. Fortunately she managed to catch her breath and slow it down before she melted completely.

'Let's get on with the job shall we?' David gave a wicked grin and pulled her gently towards the bottom of the corridor in the direction of her mother's room.

The door was open when they got there and a small round woman was just walking out of it. She stopped and beamed at them, only to be interrupted by a torrent of shouting before she had a chance to say a word.

'I'm not going anywhere, you'll take all my things, you

thieving buggers!'

'I have tried telling her,' said the round woman in hushed tones pulling the door almost shut behind her, 'But she's not in the best of moods I'm afraid.'

'Thank you Brigid,' said David with a smile, 'I'm sure it'll all be fine.'

Did he wink at her? Minerva took a deep breath and strode past both of them into the room. 'There you are, Mother,' she said in a business-like manner, 'What's the matter?'

'Who's that?' Cybele Crafty sat perched on the bed clutching at her frame, 'Piss off!'

'Oh mother please...it's me, Minerva.'

'What do you want?' She banged the metal frame as hard as she could on the floor.

'Shall we get going, Mother? We're here to take you out for a while.'

'Taking me out?' said Cybele, 'What for?'

Minerva shot a nervous glance at David.

'Cybele,' he said, 'I must say, you're looking very well. It's David by the way, remember me?'

She pulled the frame nearer and screwed her face up in his direction, 'Of course I remember, you idiot! You're the doctor. I've had enough of those too, they're all bloody liars. I don't want any more pills! I don't need them, not when it's my last day on earth...'

'What are you talking about?' said Minerva.

'You heard! It's my last day on earth. I'll be dead tomorrow.'

'There's no need for talk like that Cybele,' said David, 'You're the picture of good health.'

Cybele cackled to herself, 'Not bad for a hundred wouldn't you say?'

'You're not a hundred Mother, you know that!'

'Don't you tell me what I'm not! I've had a letter from the queen.'

'Where is it then? You can't have got a letter from the queen, you're ninety one not a hundred!'

'Shall we get going ladies?' said David looking at his watch, 'There'll be plenty of time for chatting back at Crafty Cottage.'

'I know that voice from somewhere,' said Cybele screwing her face in the direction of David's dulcet tones.

'And you'd be correct Cybele, I give the weekly service in the common room.'

So that's how he knows the carer, thought Minerva.

'What service?' asked Cybele.

'The church service, it's my job if you remember?'

'You're the vicar then,' said Cybele slowly, 'And you're taking me out to church?'

'No Mother,' said an exasperated Minerva, 'We are taking you to mine, to Crafty Cottage. David and I are together. *You know that*!'

'I don't know anything of the sort!' snapped the old woman struggling to get up, 'I need the loo.'

She pushed herself up from the bed, onto the frame and hobbled to the bathroom.

Minerva felt a twinge of horror when she thought about Crafty Cottage… her mother would never make it up the stairs which meant she would have to sleep downstairs in the living room - it was the only place to put her. She could feel the sway of the oncoming ripples across her millpond and steadied herself on the dressing table.

'Is anyone there? I need a hand!'

What awful screeching. She was going to need earplugs.

'Would that be the hand of God or the hand of the devil?' Minerva called to the half open door.

'Minerva,' warned David, with a frown.

'She can't hear me,' hissed Minerva, 'Besides, I shall need to keep myself amused somehow...you can't blame me David. Freedom of speech will be the only unrestricted thing I'll have!'

'Don't make it harder for yourself,' he said, 'I'm sure you can get on better with a little more give and take. Try and look at it as an opportunity to patch up old wounds if you can.'

Minerva couldn't. She could only see a pillow, the perfect weapon, there on the bed.

He took her hand and squeezed it.

'I said I need a hand!' screeched the voice from the bathroom.

'I'm coming!' Minerva screeched back, 'A little patience wouldn't go amiss, Mother!'

David thought about the hand of God and the hand of the devil and wondered if, in this case, there was any difference between them.

Only time and the great virtue of patience, would tell.

7

On the Edge

'Ronnie picked her way through the boxes and bags to the old armchair. After the morning she'd had, it was time for a rest. The extra walk to the village nursery always did her good; and she enjoyed the scenic route with the view of the water on the one side and the fields and hedgerows spreading out on the other. Morrigan loved it too, cooing with delight at the familiar sight of the crows, hopping and swooping and talking to her. The child was a sorceress and it was obvious the crow dancing was for no one else but the miniature warrior queen in her chariot.

The dogs loved the toddler too, and since they'd all moved in together, were never far from her side. They followed her on the boat as she led them a merry dance up and down its narrow corridors, stopping at regular intervals to inspect some new and interesting thing to play with. Their usual toys paled into insignificance when there, in the flesh, was a live and interacting one *and* she was so easy to train. All they had to do was plop the ball down at her feet and she threw it, continually. Hours of entertainment! These small humans were great fun.

The boat had unsettled Ronnie at first, living in such a confined space took some getting used to. The combination of an excited toddler and two boisterous spaniels was enough to jangle anyone's nerves and she found herself more watchful of her daughter than ever.

Sinking down into the old chair she rubbed the white, cat hair - finely pressed onto the frayed holes of the arm rests – between her fingers. The cat had lived here for a long time according to Joe, and she wondered where it was now. Prompted by the thought, she took her coffee and made her way out onto the deck at the back of the boat to join Freya. Maybe she would know where the cat was; after all, she had two of her own pulling that chariot of hers.

Ronnie looked up at the Goddess charging across the top of the open doors and wondered. She wondered what she would say to her if she could talk. She wondered if the blue beasts could find the missing boat cat and also, if she was going mad. The more she thought about it the more light headed she felt and before long she was tingling all over. The lightness was spreading through the rest of her body and fighting to stay in it she walked around and concentrated on every physical sensation she had, but it was no good...she was drifting.

What was that?

She turned to look in the direction of a strange cry coming from the water. An orange buoy bobbed up and down but there was something on it making the noise. She narrowed her eyes to get a better focus.

It was an animal. A cat.

It was Ropey's cat, there in front of her, mewing and clinging on for its life. How had it got there? She had to do something. Looking around, Ronnie saw that the buoy was two, maybe three feet away from the boat. Perhaps she could stretch across and reach it if she tried.

The cries continued.

She couldn't bear to see or hear any animal suffer – she had to try and rescue it. She jumped up onto the wooden bench on deck and onto the fencing around the top of it. Climbing partly back down on the other side she decided to lean across and try and grab the animal.

As a naturally talented horse rider, she was blessed with good balance, which she needed now more than ever. She straddled the top of the fencing as if she were mounting a horse, placing her right foot as carefully as she could onto the ledging on the far side. The water lapped at the side of the boat and the buoy began to bob furiously as the cat's high pitched cries got louder.

Gripping onto the ledge with her left hand, Ronnie pushed all thoughts of fear to the back of her mind. Nausea swept over her but she ignored it. She had to. She wasn't going to fall in. She repeated the words over in her mind as she steadied herself before fixing her gaze on the distressed animal, bobbing up and down madly on the buoy. She breathed in deep and leaned across as far as she could towards the poor creature, trying not to look down. It wasn't beyond her reach, if she could just lean a little further...stretch a bit more.

Don't look down, whatever happens, don't do that.

The water would not be kind to her and why would it be? She couldn't swim. Her mother said it was carried over from a past life and couldn't possibly be anything to do with this one, she was far too brave to be afraid of water. It must've been the ducking stool.

When her foot slipped, she panicked and lost her balance as

the water consumed her quickly and easily. Fear was a dish best served with plenty of struggle and thrashing against it did nothing to stop its hunger. It just made it worse. It wanted her and the more she struggled the hungrier it became. She opened her mouth to scream but nothing came out. Not a sound.

The water filled her lungs and pulled her down - gushing and pouring into her ears, her nose and her mouth - swallowing all of her. And she let it, she surrendered. She stopped struggling. It was easier.

The sheer force of it sucked her into a tunnel. Deeper and further she went...down into a black hole. Everything was slowing down, becoming quieter. She was drifting further and the gentle sway of the water lulled her along until the dead weight of her limbs lifted and she was floating, carried by the sheer volume of water through the misty tunnel. And gradually, as it became clearer and brighter she felt a comforting numbness...an incredible sense of peace.

Held still in the murky soup she saw streams of light pouring into the tunnel and she found herself drawn towards it effortlessly. Lasers of rainbow light spun out and around her body. She watched and felt the colours seeping into every cell, filtering through every fibre of her being until she was completely filled with light. She bathed in the glow and the warmth of it. The bliss of it.

She heard music all around her. Music like nothing on earth, the purest and sweetest sound of a thousand voices...angels singing. The melody carried her, moving her forwards to the steady pulse of a distant drum. The beat of a loving heart. The earth was alive and speaking to her and she was dancing, spinning slowly, turning into a song with her body. But the song didn't have any words, although she knew what it was saying.

Was this heaven?

Still moving towards an expanding and brighter light she noticed the darker shape of a form moving towards her. A familiar smell reached her, a velvety warmth pushed into her hands. A weight leaned against her, thick fur nudging and pressing against her skin...warm breath meeting hers. She reached out and caught an ear, running her hand to the base and further down, tracing along bone and fur. The hair of a thick and matted mane, hung down and caught her fingers. Beneath the coarse fur was warm muscle, and there it was...that smell again. The smell of horse.

It was Bob, she could feel him. The angels were singing him to life and bringing him to her. Just by thinking about it she was on his back, journeying through a mass of vibrant colour to sunshine where the surrounding fields of the most exquisite shades of green and gold pulsated with life. The smell of horse and earth filled her lungs and the soft pounding of hooves beat against ground she couldn't see. But she wasn't dreaming.

Bob was alive.

They were together again.

And there was Morrigan...running and hopping and skipping as the crows danced in circles around her. Bob stopped and began to graze. She felt a surge of love so big she couldn't contain it, or the tears. Her daughter turned to look at her and in the distance, another figure approached them. It was Joe. He stopped when he saw the tiny child and they laughed and played together. The crows joined in, applauding with shiny black wings, swooping and cawing.

Bob carried on walking past them all and she signalled him

to stop, but he wouldn't. Her heart became heavy and she felt a sensation pulling her back. Sliding down from the horse, she clung onto the thick fur but he wouldn't stop and yet she saw herself, another part of her, still with him and riding him away. She needed to find the others, the urgency to return was overwhelming and pulled her back in their direction. But they weren't there. Only an empty field and a single crow calling out…

Go back! Go back! Go back!

A whooshing sound in her ears, filling her body - pulling her backwards. She was travelling again. Back into the rainbow light, carried by the song of a thousand angels, back into the dark and narrowing space. Faster. Heading towards the light and getting brighter. She heard a muffled sound….a voice...getting louder.

'Ron! Ronnie!'

Joe.

She was struggling against heaviness, fighting for breath as something pulled her out of the water and onto the hard surface of land.

She gasped as her body heaved in spasms and belched water, 'Joe!'

'I'm here Ron, I'm here...it's all right.'

He was holding her. 'I got you, I got you Ron. It's okay...take it easy. Just breathe.'

The sunlight was blinding but she was desperate to see his face. And there it was…unsmiling, eyes staring…but his strong arms around her, holding her tight.

Don't let go. Don't let me go.

She clung to him and he squeezed her.

They were locked together, speechless. Joe let out a heavy

sigh, 'That was a close one Ron.' His breath was warm on her neck.

She spluttered, her own breath returning in shallow gasps, 'Was it?'

'Jesus, it was lucky I saw you. I was just coming back for a cuppa'. If I hadn't of been here I don't know what –'

She hung onto his warm body. 'The cat,' she murmured, 'It was the cat.'

Joe looked at her, 'What do you mean, the cat?'

'The boat cat, Ropey's cat. It was stuck out on the water.'

'No, that wasn't Ropey's cat. Can't have been. I've just been talking to them in the chandlery about that. They said someone found it washed up on the slipway last week. Dead.'

'No,' said Ronnie, 'I saw it. Tried to rescue it, that's what I was doing! It was the cat we saw on the boat the other day!'

Joe was looking at her strangely, 'Are you sure? It could've been *another* cat.'

'I *know* what I saw and it was Ropey's cat, stuck on that buoy, by the boat.'

She held up her hand and pointed weakly towards the boat and the orange buoy on the far side of it.

'Let's get you into some dry clothes,' he spoke briskly while gently lifting her up.

'You don't believe me.'

'Ron, all I can believe at the moment is you're here in one piece. You're alive and it could've been a lot different, but you're here. And what I *do* know for certain - you are learning to swim. And I'm going to teach you...as soon as you're recovered.'

He held her to him and they clung to each other. She closed her eyes and saw the cat on the buoy. She felt Bob's body, still warm beneath hers. She heard Morrigan's high pitched giggle and angels singing.

Was any of it real? She pulled at her sodden t-shirt. It wasn't a dream.

'Come on,' said Joe, taking the weight of her, 'Let's get you home and dry.'

It sounded like a good idea. She was exhausted.

* * *

Staring at the pile of wet clothes she pulled the warm towel closer to her tired body.

'Here, this'll do you good.'

Joe handed her the steaming mug and watched her.

'Jesus,' she spluttered.

'Nice bit of rum that,' said Joe, 'Goes well with the tea...'

'I'm not sure about that, it's burning my mouth!'

'Put a fire in your belly that will - just what you need!'

'Is it?' she said, peering over the rim of her mug at him, 'I'm not sure any more.'

'What's up?'

'What happened is what's up. I went somewhere, Joe...'

He laughed softly, 'Yeah, you did. Over the side of the bloody boat and nearly drowned! Where else could you've gone?'

Ronnie looked out over the water, 'I don't know, it was like a dream but it felt so real.'

'All right, tell me...' he said, 'But that can't have been Ropey's cat you saw. I told you, I'd just been in the chandlery and they said that someone found it on the slipway just the other day, drowned.'

'...And I'm telling *you* I know what I saw. It was the same cat we saw on the boat the other day. It was Ropey's cat!'

Joe sat back and stared at her, 'Well that's bloody weird if you ask me. A dead cat can't be in two places at once can it?'

Ronnie shrugged and took a gulp of her drink, 'Maybe it can.'

'What are you saying? That you saw a ghost or something?'

'I don't know, I wish I did,' she sighed, 'Truth is, I saw a lot of things down there in the water.'

'Go on…'

'It was surreal. I went through a tunnel. It was dark but I didn't feel scared or anything, in fact, I felt safe. There was a beautiful light with all colours weaving in and out of it – a bit like a kaleidoscope I suppose. And then singing, the most exquisite songs you ever heard...'

Joe raised his eyebrows.

'It was like...' she hesitated, 'A heavenly choir.'

'Of angels?'

'Yes, angels,' she said leaning into him, 'No other word for it.'

'Then what?'

'Then I saw Bob. I smelt him and then I could feel him, it was so *real*. We travelled, me and Bob, through the most amazing landscape…the colours were –'

'–psychedelic?'

She narrowed her eyes at him, 'Yes they were...and the music carried on all around us. And then I saw you and Morrigan playing in a field with some crows. But you didn't see me or Bob, it's like we were invisible. I wanted to stop but Bob just carried on going and I jumped off and tried to find you but there was only one crow left in the field, and you and Morrigan had gone, disappeared. I wanted to find you both, but then I was pulled back through the tunnel, past all the same things again and then you were pulling me out of the water….'

'I wasn't on a white charger by any chance?' he said, winking at her, 'Quite partial to the odd damsel in distress.'

'Joe!' she nudged him hard with her shoulder, 'I told you what happened, it's the truth!'

'I don't doubt it Ron, really I don't. Are you sure you hadn't been at my hash tin beforehand?'

'No! I'd just got back from dropping Morrigan off at playschool. I don't touch your stuff, you know I don't. It doesn't do anything for me...'

'Yeah I know. You've definitely got your own thing going on. Hey…' he stopped. 'What if that was one of those near death things?'

'Do you think so?'

'Well, you were definitely on the edge weren't you? How long do you reckon you were down there for?'

'I have no idea. It's strange, because it felt like forever but I know it can't have been can it? How long can anyone last underwater before —'

'— they're dead meat? Probably only about four minutes, tops. Then the brain gets starved of oxygen and if you come back after that…well, let's just say it's better that you don't.'

Ronnie stared at him, 'But it felt much longer than four minutes...more like four hours! It was like being outside of time. Mum talks about it when she does her hedge riding.'

'What the hell's that?'

'She goes over the hedge and travels into another world. The spirit world.'

'Over the edge more like. You mean on some journey?'

'Yes, kind of. I told you it was like a dream but I feel so different after it.'

'Yeah, sounds about right. You couldn't experience something like that without being changed in some way could you?'

She'd been somewhere beyond any kind of dream world, she just wasn't sure where.

'Are you okay?' he squeezed her shoulders, 'Why don't you lie down for a while, get some rest and I'll go pick up Morrigan later and take her round your Mum's for a while. Get some sleep eh? You need it.'

She nodded. She did feel exhausted – her body felt like a dead weight - and yet in another way, she felt more alive than ever. Is this what happened to almost dead people when they came back?

'Yes,' she murmured, 'Thanks.'

'No need to thank me,' he said, steering her to the bedroom, 'Anything for you, you know that...'

His voice was the anchor she needed right now. Everything was all right. *They* were all right. Morrigan was all right. And Bob, out there somewhere...he was all right too.

It was a comforting thought.

Sleep came quickly.

8

Green Man and Babycham

Minerva woke up with a start. Was that Lucifer crying outside? As the sound got louder and the prodding from behind became more urgent, she turned towards the bedroom door. David was pushing hard against her and unable to ignore either for any longer she forced herself out of bed with a groan.

The noise was coming from the living room. With a sinking feeling she grabbed her dressing gown and felt her way down the stairs towards the noise. As she opened the door a dark shape emerged.

'Who's that?' said the dark shape, 'Is anyone there?'

Minerva fumbled for the light switch, 'Mother, what are you doing? What's the matter?'

The pink and wrinkled figure in the doorway reminded her of one of those frozen mice she used to get from the pet shop for her snake, Baldrick. Like the mice, Baldrick was long dead now, but her mother wasn't. Yet. 'Where are your clothes?'

'I want my shower, are you going to give me my shower?'

'Not at this time of the morning, Mother, no,' said Minerva, averting her eyes from the naked body to the clock on the wall, 'It's half past three for heaven's sake!'

'I don't sleep. I *told* you I don't sleep. You might as well give me my shower now that you're up.'

Minerva's fists tightened inside the pockets of her dressing gown. Weren't people supposed to wake *up* from nightmares, not in them?

'It's far too early to be thinking about showers yet Mother, please..! Come on,' she said, steering the naked Cybele back through the door, 'Let's get your nightdress on and back to bed, before you catch pneumonia.'

'Aren't you going to make me a cup of tea?'

* * *

Minerva stared trance like at the kettle, waiting for it to boil. How quickly life could change. Having her granddaughter to care for was nothing compared with a ninety one year old who's only joy seemed to be antagonizing every person in her orbit. Especially Minerva.

As the water bubbled she wondered how long it would last. How long could she stand this untimely and rude interruption in her life? She looked at the jars of herbs and resisted the urge to reach for the belladonna. Perhaps a drop of brandy might be the safer option for now. She found the bottle and poured a generous amount of alcohol onto the bobbing tea bags. It would do both of them a favour. Her mother needed to sleep and she needed to forget.

Next to the kettle she noticed the red velvet bag tucked behind a jar of coffee. Automatically she reached for it, took out her Tarot cards and shuffled them with the swiftness and ease of one who'd mastered their craft. She'd never lost her fascination for the silky cards with the bright and magical pictures and still used the same deck her aunt Crow had given her when she was a girl. Somehow the symbols had always been familiar, speaking to her like an old friend through every sword and cup, wand and pentacle. She trusted them.

She smiled at the Nine of Pentacles, a card of self-employment. How significant. It was true, she enjoyed her work with the cards and a lifetime of study had developed into a decent living. Minerva had never enjoyed working for anyone else. Rules and regulations were a noose around the neck and being told what to do by anyone else served only to tighten it. She stroked her throat while looking deeper into the picture at the snail and the bird of prey. The snail was the voice of reason and persistence while the bird of prey signified visionary power and achievement. It was a fair portrayal. I've certainly worked for what I have, thought Minerva.

'Are you still there?'

And there's my next job.

Minerva put the card back in the deck, stuffed them into the red bag and returned to the front room, scowling.

'Where is your nightdress, Mother?' she said through gritted teeth, putting down the mugs as quietly as she could. David mustn't be disturbed.

'How would I know?' said the pink and wrinkly figure stooping over the walking frame, 'I can't find the damn bed, where is it?'

'Right in front of you, look!'

Her mother banged the frame defiantly against the floor. 'Don't you tell me to look when I can't see, you know I can't!'

As she wrestled with the grumbling mound of wobbling bare

flesh Minerva told herself that dressing a ninety-one year old was not unlike dressing a two-year old.

'There now, please try and be quiet Mother. It's very early, so drink your tea and try and get some sleep.'

'I told you, I don't sleep, never have...don't you listen?'

Minerva didn't answer, preferring to sip her tea in silence, focusing on the liquid fire as it trickled into her belly.

'That's right, always too wrapped up in yourself and what *you* wanted.'

Minerva continued to ignore her. She wasn't going to fuel her mother's need for conflict if she could help it.

Her mother coughed and spluttered, 'What's *this?* Trying to poison me are you?'

'It won't hurt, Mother. It'll help relax you. I've got some in my tea.'

'What is it? Bloody rocket fuel?. You're trying to finish me off with one of your weird concoctions.'

'Not this time, I'm afraid. Thank you for the suggestion though, I shall keep it for future reference.'

'You won't have to. I shall save you the bother. It's my last day on earth.'

'What makes you so sure? You've been saying that for ages and you're still here.'

'Not for much longer you'll be pleased to hear.'

'Well, do you think you could hurry up and get on with it then? I haven't got all day.'

'I'll go when I'm good and ready.'

'Oh, that's how it works is it?'

The door creaked open to reveal a bleary-eyed David, 'Is everything all right?' he said, peering at Minerva. She could see he was wearing her old dressing gown which looked far better on him than it did on her.

'Who's that?' said Cybele, straining to see over her frame, 'I know that voice from somewhere.'

David yawned, 'It's me, Cybele...David. We've met on many occasions at Prickly Hall if you remember? The weekly church service?

Cybele screwed her face up at him, 'What are you doing here then? I told you it was my last day on earth,' she turned to Minerva, 'He's sent someone.'

'Who's *he*?' said Minerva signalling for David to come and sit down.

'Who do you think? God of course!'

How very typical of her mother to think he'd been sent for her. She *would* think that. And why was David laughing, at this unearthly hour?

'I'm not actually the man himself but it's very nice of you to say so Cybele,' he glanced sideways at Minerva, 'But I'm sure you're right...he's closer than you think.'

'I don't think, I *know*.'

'Yes of course Mother, you would.' She looked at David, 'Cup of tea?'

He nodded and squeezed her arm. It would take more than that to pacify her, she thought, as she poured another healthy dose of brandy into her tea. Quickly, she reached for the red bag again and picked a card, or rather it picked her. Out flipped the Page of Pentacles, portrayed as the daughter of earth.

Oh yes, she was that all right, grounded in every way.

But how would she cope? David was right by her side, of that she was certain. But he had his job to get on with and couldn't hold her hand the whole time could he? She made a hazy mental note to find her spell book later and get to work on something. It was magic or murder. The question was could a daughter of the earth kill her own mother? Certainly not with a vicar in the house. Plotting was a job for the solitary Witch.

She would just have to bide her time.

* * *

Isis looked up at the clock on the wall. Pushing the silky hairpiece back into a central position she secured it as best she could with a shaking hand. Her eyes darted around the walls of the Old Druid and stopped at a bundle of brown edged carnations in a jar of cloudy water.

Everything would be fine. Gerald would be there at any moment. But had she forgotten something? Feeling for the thin chain and silver angel around her neck, she closed her eyes for a moment and sighed as she held it. Minerva had given it to her, she said it would remind her of her guardian angel, ever present and always around. It was a great comfort.

She stroked the smooth and tiny figure, her lips moving without sound, *Make me calm....please!*

She kissed the angel and slipped it under her top, patting it with a clammy hand. Looking around the empty pub to the large wooden door on the far side she caught her breath as it creaked open to reveal the tall and sun-kissed Gerald beaming a radiant smile across the room.

Isis glanced behind her. There was nobody else there.

'That was for you,' said Gerald, bending down to kiss her, 'And so is this...'

Isis fluttered for a second, her heart beating so loud she could feel it pounding in her mouth against his as she forced her eyes to stay shut. After the kiss which seemed to linger for ever she pulled the thin silk of her harem pants away from sweaty skin and the hard chair beneath her.

'A nice cold drink?'

'Er yes, yes please. Anything cold would be good...thank you.'

He smiled at her again, 'Soft drink or a drop of the hard stuff? What do you fancy?'

Taking her sweating hand, he bent to kiss it, 'Your wish is my command, sweet Isis.'

She'd never been treated like royalty before.

'A Babycham would be very nice if that's all right?'

'Of course it is. My pleasure!'

She watched him glide over to the bar and casually chat to Ernie as he served the drinks. Gerald possessed such an air of confidence, it positively oozed out of him. So how could it be that someone so comfortable in his own skin could have quite the opposite effect on one who wasn't? Isis shifted uneasily in her seat and focused hard on her breathing. The more she tried to control it the worse it seemed to get, so that when Gerald came back, Isis had turned a dark shade of beetroot and appeared to be hyperventilating.

'Isis, whatever is the matter? You look uncomfortable to say the least.'

'I'm just a bit hot that's all,' panted Isis.

'I'm not surprised, it's extremely stuffy in here,' said Gerald, looking around the room, 'Not a window open anywhere. Shall we venture outside and get some fresh air? I know it's a warm day but at least there's something to breathe out there!'

He offered a strong, suntanned arm and Isis took it gladly, allowing him to lead the way outside into the beer garden around the back. They parked themselves beneath the cherry blossom tree and sat in silence for a while. Isis appreciated the quiet, it gave her space to breathe beneath the tree's steadying influence.

'Thank you Gerald,' she said, finding her breath. 'Sometimes my nerves get the better of me...it's almost like they have a mind of their own!'

Gerald laughed, 'I think you'll find that you have more control than you think you do Isis. Have you tried any kind of relaxation techniques?'

'What?' Isis looked up from the swiftly diminishing Babycham, 'I do Belly dancing if that counts. Minerva and I go every week and we love it.'

'And that's a wonderful thing I'm sure,' said Gerald, 'But is it only women who go?'

Isis looked down at her peppermint espadrilles, 'Why yes. I can't imagine a man doing what we do, although I suppose they could do it. In fact they probably do, I'm sure they do. What are you getting at?'

'Only that perhaps you're not as used to being in the company of men as you are women.' Gerald's voice hushed to a whisper, 'Would that be true?'

'I suppose mainly and on the whole, yes,' said Isis, looking away. 'Women are generally more friendly and trustworthy, in my experience anyway. I was married to a man who was none of those things and extremely controlling. It left me quite a shadow of my former self to be frank.'

'Ah yes, I'm getting the picture.'

'It's one I'm trying to forget.'

'But the body remembers...'

'Does it?'

'Yes it does. And it can hold onto those memories too, but

only if you let it.'

Isis gave him a puzzled look.

'Once you know that on a conscious level, when you are aware of what is going on, you can really do something about it.'

'Really?'

'Yes, really, Isis. Mind over matter is what many call it, or, as I prefer to call it; Magic over the mundane. You can achieve anything you want when you get your head in the right place.'

'That's what Minerva's always saying,' smiled Isis, *'The magical mindset is the key.'*

'Yes, the magical nature is above and beyond the comprehension of most of us lesser mortals, but in simple terms - we make real what we believe in. And when the magician grasps the power in those words he can achieve anything...as indeed can *you*. If you can believe in yourself, *nothing* is impossible. Believe me.'

Isis watched him as he rose to stand by the tree, deftly removing their empty glasses from the table in one hand. She blinked hard as his body seemed to merge with the trunk, becoming one with it, his legs disappearing slowly into the ground until there was no physical evidence of the man left at all. For a split second he was gone and just as she felt a wave of panic threatening to return, so did Gerald, fully formed again in the flesh.

'What happened there? Where did you go?'

Gerald smiled, 'Oh just a bit of shape-shifting…and some tree alchemy to ground and lighten the spirit!'

'Spirit? I'll have another Babycham please.'

She pinched herself under the table. Having one's very own Green Man was going to take a bit of getting used to.

The second Babycham slipped down better than the first and Isis began to feel less jittery. A warm feeling in her stomach began to spread around her body as she thought about Gerald's godliness. There was the earthly side of the man - whose physical presence was so grounded to the earth he was one with it - and there was the *unearthly*, where he seemed to become part of another world. A magical world.

He made her feel like a Goddess. He *had* to be a God. No man could have that effect on a woman without coming from somewhere else.

Gerald squeezed her hand, 'So anyway, how is your good friend Minerva these days?'

It was a while before she answered and he never prompted her once, but sat there holding her hand and beaming at her.

'That's a God question, I *mean* a good question...' giggled Isis, 'She's facing quite a challenge at the moment - her mother is staying with her. She's elderly, in her nineties and not the easiest of people to care for. She puts on a brave face but I think Minerva is finding it a bit of a strain to be honest.

'Good for her,' said Gerald, 'I cared for my dear grandmother just before she left this mortal world and it was an absolute privilege – I can see that now – although at the time it wasn't always apparent, but she was quite delightful really.'

'I don't think that's how Minerva would describe her mother at all,' said Isis. 'From what I can gather, and what I've seen, Cybele is quite a force to be reckoned with and definitely not a delight in Minerva's eyes. Maybe things will change.'

'Oh they will,' said Gerald with great certainty, 'They always do. Life has a way of working out and better for some than others if you know what I mean?'

No she didn't. The last time she'd seen Minerva, she was

at her wits end and Isis couldn't imagine that was going to change any time soon.

'I'm not sure I do know what you mean,' said Isis, looking straight at him.

'Minerva is a practitioner of the magical arts, isn't she?'

'You mean a Witch?

'Well yes, if we must talk labels,' he peered at her from under the brim of his hat, 'then *that* is what I mean.'

'So, how will the way of a Witch change her current situation?'

Gerald held up his hand and stopped her in her tracks. She could feel his strength and mastery. Here was a man who knew his own power and it was intoxicating. She was drinking him in. It was exciting and scary at the same time but she didn't care. He knew what he was doing.

All masters did.

'The *way of the Witch,* as you call it dear Isis, is as old as time. Weaving back and forth and in and out of time and space is what we do to create our magic. And it is the art itself of weaving and working the energy upon and within ourselves that for the most part creates the biggest changes. The Witch is skilled in this ancient wisdom and her craft is the *practise* of it. It's how the old becomes the new again and again.'

'Yes, I suppose so,' replied Isis beginning to fidget. 'When you put it like that, it all sounds very believable. Minerva is just under a bit of strain at the moment with other things on her mind. I'm sure she'll get back to it in no time.'

'I would go as far to say she has never left it at all. But yes, at the moment the mundane could be outweighing the magical by some distance. Perhaps she could do with a reminder, what about we pay her a visit or better still, take her out?'

'Oh yes, I'm sure she could do with a change of scenery and a bit of time away from her mother,' said Isis. 'Respite they call it, don't they?'

'I believe they do,' smiled Gerald, 'Time off from the burden of such a responsibility is something which shouldn't be ignored or forgotten about.'

'You're absolutely right,' said Isis, 'How kind of you to think of Minerva's situation in that way. She'll be thrilled I'm sure. I'll get in touch with Ronnie and ask her to sit with her grandmother for a few hours, I'm sure she'll happily oblige. Where did you have in mind?'

Gerald stared into the distance, stroking his chin with long brown fingers, 'Perhaps an afternoon out in the woods, bluebells are rampant at the moment...' he said, before turning to Isis, 'I know just the place, it backs onto my bungalow.'

'Oh I'd like that, I mean, *Minerva* will like that!' she gushed. 'It sounds like a wonderful idea.'

'And a magical one I hope,' said Gerald, 'I'm sure we can make it so...'

Isis flung her arms around his broad shoulders and kissed him, 'It will be lovely, *you're lovely!* Now I can't wait to tell her what's on the cards although if I know Minerva, she probably knows already!

Isis laughed girlishly before sinking into his embrace.

'Yes,' pondered Gerald, stroking her hairpiece. 'She probably does.'

9

Hocus Pocus

Ronnie loved to hear Morrigan laughing. How she delighted in good company!

Today it was Joe and the dogs, bounding and bouncing from one side of her to the other as Ronnie fought to keep control of a buggy straining to hold the wriggling and giggling two year old. As they ventured through the corn field, Ronnie concentrated hard to avoid the large cracks in the ground while Morrigan took great delight in the bumpy ride, the sun on her face and the enthusiasm of her four-legged companions.

'Let her out for a bit, shall we Ron?' called Joe from the front of the entourage.

'We're late already,' said Ronnie, glancing at her phone. 'Mum said she's going out at two and it's almost that now!'

'Oh come on, don't be a *spoil sport,*' shouted Joe. 'We're having fun aren't we guys?!'

The spaniels bounced around in unison while Morrigan let out a squeal of impatience, pushing against the confines of the buggy straps with outstretched arms.

'Looks like you're out-voted Ron...the small Goddess cries

freedom!'

'You don't have to tell me that,' said Ronnie, wrestling with the unwieldy buggy.

'Unchain her then! Let her play, just until we get to the road eh? It'll do her good, get rid of a bit of her energy before we get to your mum's...'

He leapt around the dogs and jumped to a dramatic standstill in front of the swaying buggy.

'Who do you think you are?' she laughed, 'Robin Hood?'

'Aha! Glad to see you've lightened up my Lady.'

He removed his hat and bowed deeply, sending waves of golden brown curls springing out from the faded baseball cap.

'Well, it's kind of difficult not to be, with you around.'

'Nice of you to say so m'Lady, must be the company I keep!'

Unhooking the buggy straps, he picked Morrigan up and put her down with familiar ease. Buggies and babies and boyfriends didn't always go together - especially if the baby was someone else's - but Ronnie was fortunate and she knew it.

'Not too long now Joe, I don't want to keep Mum waiting. She deserves some time off from Gran...'

'Yeah you're right,' said Joe quickening his pace in front of the empty buggy while Morrigan toddled frantically to keep up with the dogs, 'How about you leave the buggy and go ahead? Then you can get to your mum's sooner and we'll see you later.'

Morrigan had stopped to inspect a butterfly and was now sidling off the path into the corn after it. Without hesitation, the dogs disappeared among the towering stalks to join her. And so the game of hide and seek began.

'Actually, that'd be great,' said Ronnie, 'I'll leave her bag in the buggy here. There's a drink and some food if she wants it.'

Joe took the buggy, kissed her and waved her past him, 'Off you go m'Lady!'

She smiled before calling back, 'And the baby wipes! They're in the bag...in case she gets dirty!'

'Anyone'd think it was an overnight job! We'll see you later on, okay?'

Joe had already disappeared into the corn while Ronnie, with a lightness in her stride, headed in the direction of the village. Opening her arms wide and breathing in the last of the hawthorn still scattering the hedges, she marched onwards to Crafty Cottage where her mother was waiting. Looking after her grandmother for a few hours would make a nice change.

She was looking forward to the break.

* * *

'Are you sure you can't make it? It would be so nice if you could come too, David!' Minerva whined down the phone.

'I know it would, but I can't get out of this meeting with the bishop of the diocese...it's one of those fixtures in the diary that can't be *un-fixed* Minerva, you know that. You'll have a great time with Isis and her new beau, I'm sure!'

'Hmm, I can't help thinking what a prize gooseberry I shall feel like, stuck between the pair of them.'

'I don't think that'll be the case at all,' said David in his usual calming tone. 'There goes your imagination running away again.'

'Well, it's the *only* thing that's running away with me. Perhaps if it weren't for your other engagement, it might be you!'

She couldn't help it. The re-emergence of her inner child was all her mother's fault.

'Minerva, enough of all that,' laughed David. 'Branbury Woods is one of your favourite places – the bluebells are out too - and regardless of who you're with, you'll be in your element.'

'One of *our* favourite places if you remember.'

'Yes of course I remember, how could I forget?'

'I must go…Ronnie's just arrived. See you soon and good luck with the bishop!'

No sooner had Ronnie stepped through the front door, Isis and Gerald appeared behind her.

'I'll be with you both in one minute,' said Minerva to the unlikely pair on the doorstep before turning to Ronnie, 'Darling, she's out for the count at the moment but there's plenty of cake in the cupboard for later.'

'What about dinner? What does she have?'

'Cake, like I said...or biscuits, oh and there's some jelly in the fridge,' said Minerva, checking it was still there. 'She'll only eat something sweet so I wouldn't bother with anything else, not unless you want a battle on your hands.'

'Er, no Mum, I think I'll pass on that.'

'Very wise,' said Minerva grabbing her bag and heading for the door. 'You never know, you may even enjoy yourself and I'm sure your grandmother will appreciate the change in company. We do rub each other up the wrong way at times!'

'It'll all be fine Mum,' said Ronnie, ushering her outside. 'Just you go and enjoy yourself and tell me all about it later.'

'I will darling. You're a star, thank you!'

Minerva blew her a kiss and disappeared. Ronnie tentatively poked her head round the door in the hallway and smiled at the sight of her grandmother - feet up, head back and mouth wide open – in the front room. She almost made it to the kitchen when a voice stopped her:

'Minerva is that you? Are you there?'

'Hi Gran, it's me,' called Ronnie before darting back into the front room. 'How are you doing? Can I get you anything?'

The old woman screwed her face up in the direction of the voice, 'What? Who's that?'

'It's *me* Gran,' said Ronnie, stepping right in front of her. 'Ronnie, remember?'

'Of course I remember. What do you take me for? Old and decrepit I may be, but I haven't lost my marbles yet.'

Ronnie laughed softly, 'No I didn't think so Gran, you're much too smart for all that. Would you like a drink or something to eat? Are you hungry?'

'I'm never hungry! Haven't had an appetite for years...it's what getting old does to you.'

'Tea?'

'Yes, I'll have a cuppa'. Is there any cake?'

'I think there might be Gran. I'll go and have a look.'

'I need to go to the loo first...'

'Oh,' said Ronnie retracing her steps, 'Let me help.'

'No you won't,' grumbled her grandmother, shuffling across the room on her frame, 'I can manage. A nice piece of cake and a cuppa' did you say?'

Ronnie wondered what all the fuss was about, though her mother did have a tendency to exaggerate, especially about her gran. With tea and cake carefully balanced in each hand, she made her way back to the living room.

'So where's she gone then?' asked her grandmother, spitting cake crumbs into the air.

'You mean Mum? She's gone out with some friends...Isis and her new boyfriend. Do you know them Gran?'

'What? You need to speak up girl, I don't hear as good

nowadays!'

'Mum's gone out with Isis and...'

'Oh that soppy bitch with the daft clothes...looks like something out of the Arabian Knights.'

'Isis does have an interesting style of dressing, but she's got a heart of gold.'

'She's as daft as they come,' said her grandmother, stuffing the rest of the cake into her mouth.

Ronnie took a slow, deep breath in, 'Do you read anymore Gran? You used to love reading didn't you? I remember you reading me all those fairy stories when I was little. I loved that!'

The old woman was quiet for a moment, her expression softening, catching the last of the crumbs with her tongue, like a lizard. 'You're right, I did love to read and yes, you were a good listener - but no, I don't see well at all now. That's the way of it Rhiannon, this getting old business.'

Ronnie scanned the bookcase in the corner of the room, 'Would you like me to read to you?'

'Not any of that magic rubbish though,' spat her grandmother, a hard look creeping across her features once more, 'And that's all she's got I suppose...'

'Well that's where you're wrong Gran,' said Ronnie, pulling out a white hardback with *Voices of Angels* in silver lettering down the spine. 'I think this might do the job.'

The old woman screwed her nose up and popped out her false teeth before sucking them back in again, 'What's it about then? No fornicating faeries or gory goblins I hope.'

Ronnie thought she saw a glimmer of light in her grandmother's eye, 'Actually no, you'll be disappointed to hear it's about angels...a bit tame in comparison. Shall I put it back?'

'Angels eh? The vicar used to mention them every week at church. I suppose they're closer to God than those wretched faeries. What is it, a story?'

'It's a whole book of different stories Gran, but they're all true,' she said glancing at the inside of the book. 'Stories about people who have seen angels and heard them, talked with them even...sounds quite fascinating doesn't it?'

'I don't know if I actually *believe* in them. Do you? *I've* never seen one.'

Ronnie sat down next to the armchair with the book on her lap and placed her hand over the bent up fingers of her grandmother.

'I'm not so sure that seeing *is* believing, Gran.'

'Don't you go all hocus pocus on me now! What do you mean?'

'Only that sometimes maybe we don't have to see them to believe they're real and that maybe they talk to us in different ways,' she said, opening the book. 'Shall we read it and find out? I'm game if you are...'

'Speak up and get on with it then.'

Ronnie suppressed a smile, cleared her throat and turned to the first chapter.

As Joe would say, *everything was groovy.*

10

Woods and Angels

Minerva breathed in the fresh, woodland air and gazed in awe at the scene around her. Freedom at last. There was nothing quite like the magic of nature to enchant and soothe the soul. This is *wonderful,* she thought, as they trudged in single file along the path through the trees and ferns; each in their own silent world. She could literally feel the tension draining from her body, every step lighter than the last. The thick carpet of bluebells shimmered among the tall, ivory bones of the silver birches; a tree she had always loved. The remains of the hawthorn lingered, its sweet perfume filling the warm air...one final performance before the arrival of summer.

I will never tire of this, thought Minerva as a Woodpecker knocked urgently through the trees. 'There goes nature's very own DJ,' she said dreamily, 'I do love this time of year don't you Isis?'

'DJ? What do you mean?'

Isis was always eager to learn more about the symbolism in nature.

'That Woodpecker, do you hear him?' Minerva stopped and pointed at the trees in the distance, 'There he goes on a continuous loop, over and over...'

Isis cocked her head with a puzzled look, 'Ah yes, I see what you mean.'

'Shall we move on ladies,' Gerald called out in a business-like manner, 'We're nearly there.'

'*Where* exactly is that?' said Minerva.

'Now that would be telling!'

Was he trying to be mysterious? It was hard to tell with someone you hadn't known for long, but there was an edge to him, something Minerva couldn't quite fathom. It was somewhere on the periphery of her consciousness, not in full view yet, but there all the same. She'd learnt to trust this mental fogginess while always giving the benefit of the doubt to the situation or person concerned. It was only fair, after all.

'That's a very impressive hamper he's carrying,' said Minerva, 'I didn't think about a picnic...but how lovely. The fresh air always gives me an appetite!'

Isis cleared her throat, 'Gerald has an appetite for *other things* as well, Minerva. Prepare to be amazed!'

Minerva narrowed her eyes at her friend, 'What *other things* would those be? Are we talking magical things?'

'We are indeed,' said Isis. 'Gerald is like you, hadn't you noticed?'

'I seem to recall him saying something about it, yes. Although as you know, I've been somewhat preoccupied with my mother, who is a complete drain apart from when she's asleep.'

'And that's why we brought you here,' beamed Isis. 'Such a good idea of Gerald's wasn't it? He's very tuned in!'

'Is he now? said Minerva, 'To what?'

'Oh you know - everything! Especially to other people, he seems to know just what they need.'

'Does that include your needs?'

'Oh yes, he's very kind to me, he really cares. This *was* his suggestion. He knows how much strain you've been under lately and he also knows you're a Witch...'

'Because you told him.'

'I didn't have to, he *knows!* You've always said that Witches recognize their own, isn't that right?'

'Yes, I know, I'm sorry Isis. I didn't mean to sound so —'

'—Suspicious?'

'I wouldn't put it *that* strongly,' said Minerva. 'Let's just say it's not a bad thing to err on the side of caution, particularly when it comes to magical matters. It's not always a good idea to trust someone completely, at least not right at the beginning.'

'Well I can assure you Minerva,' said Isis, a gentle defiance in her tone, 'Gerald has been nothing but kindness itself to me. In every way, he is the perfect gentleman.'

'I'm sure he is, Isis. I don't mean to be a stick in the mud, I'm just looking out for you, that's all. After all those years of misery with Derek, you deserve someone extra special to make up for it, don't you think?'

'Yes I do think, and I appreciate what you're saying, really I do,' whispered Isis. 'I'm a lot stronger than I used to be thanks to you and not half as daft either, I hope.'

'You're certainly not daft Isis, and I can see you're happy and I'm glad, really I am. Just be careful that's all.'

'Of what?'

'Are you two ladies ready for some magic?

Minerva glared at Isis, '*That's* what I mean,' she hissed, 'I hardly know the man and he assumes that it's okay to lead me *and you* up the garden path and do the work of the sacred art. Who does he think he is?'

'Minerva, I think you're over-reacting. There's no need to take things so seriously.'

'You know I take my magical beliefs extremely seriously, Isis!'

Isis began to flap her hands, a habit Minerva found particularly irritating. 'I didn't mean it like *that!* It's all quite understandable how, of course, anyone would be stressed out with all you've had going on. But there's no need to worry, really there isn't. Let's catch up, come on!'

Minerva took a deep breath and followed her friend in the direction of Gerald's bright chatter. What was she thinking? Isis was right, she hadn't realized how bogged down she'd become with her mother around. It was time to lighten up and enjoy herself for a change.

'Isis,' called Minerva, 'That hamper of Gerald's...'

'The answer is yes.' Isis shouted behind her, marching on ahead.

'Well, I'm very glad to hear that! The warm air does seem to make one thirsty and a drink really would do the trick right now, wouldn't you agree?'

'I would indeed,' replied Isis. 'It's the one thing I put in the hamper myself.'

'Good job. I'm impressed.'

'Thank you. And the good news is, brandy is not Gerald's tipple, so all the more for us.'

'How very shrewd of you,' said Minerva, 'I like your style.'

'Oh yes,' said Isis, pushing her hairpiece back into place. 'It's getting better all the time.'

* * *

Joe still hadn't turned up. Ronnie checked her phone but there was no message and it was already starting to get dusky. She'd long finished reading to her grandmother, who in the meantime, had polished off another two rounds of cake and jelly.

The angel stories had gone down well. So well in fact, that Ronnie had promised to do it again subject to the availability of cake and jelly and a place for Morrigan at nursery. This had pleased her grandmother, who, after an afternoon of celestial tales had promptly fallen asleep with mouth agape, teeth jutting out like a half opened drawer and was now snoring alongside the evening chorus outside.

Ronnie noticed her mother's Tarot pouch perched on the mantle piece, beside a candle. Instinctively, she lit the candle and took the cards. Pushing all conscious thoughts to the back of her mind she stared at the flickering candle as she shuffled the cards in slow motion. A card flew out from the deck and she stopped to look at it, taking note of its significance. Wild cards were especially important.

She had to smile at Temperance, it was one of her favourites. There was everything beautiful in the image: the colours of a rainbow, a glowing sunrise in the background and an angelic being – wasn't it Iris, Goddess of the rainbow? Ronnie looked up as she pondered on this, her gaze wandering to her grandmother sleeping peacefully in front of her. She blinked a number of times when a beam of light appeared behind the armchair…it was small but bright and still. It hovered above the old woman and Ronnie froze as she watched the light expand and fill the room with its radiance. She felt a chill come over the room and yet she wasn't scared.

'You're right, there's nothing to fear.'

She knew the voice was talking to her but that didn't stop her craning her neck around to see where it was coming from. Her gaze settled on the hazy light in front of her which was changing shape, taking form and growing taller.

Ronnie stiffened as the sound of soft laughter drifted towards her.

'Who are you?' she whispered.

Shielding her eyes from the brightness, she realised the form looked exactly like the image on the Tarot card she was holding.

'That's right,' said the voice so softly she could hardly hear it, 'There in your hand, is the clue. Now you need to remember what you said earlier.'

Ronnie tried to think, 'What about?

'You said you weren't sure seeing was believing. And you were right, it isn't. Your *belief* is what enables you to experience the magic of the spirit. And believing *is* receiving.'

'Is that what you are then...a spirit? Is that what angels are?'

The being didn't reply but became brighter still, pulsating in a blaze of colour.

'If it's all about belief,' said Ronnie, 'then doesn't that mean we can make up anything we want for it to be real? What about the *truth* of things?'

The angel laughed again, 'It's good to look deeply...and yes, your beliefs become your own truths for as long as you think about them, but nothing can clarify the message quite like experience – as you have encountered only recently.'

Ronnie stared at the light in front of her and felt the tingling of an electric current run through her body. Words caught in her throat and she sat motionless and stunned by the words of this celestial being, there in the room, *speaking to her.*

'That is the real difference,' said the angel, 'And what you are discovering through your own experience at this time dear Soul, is a *knowing*. This knowing is more than a mere belief…it is certainty and in certainty there is truth.

Your beliefs are from the mind and you are right when you say you can create your own truths and these do indeed become your reality. We are all creators and everything begins with thought. But knowing comes from the heart – a feeling so strong it cannot be ignored – for it is the wisdom of the Great Eternal Spirit. This has been revealed to you and you know it. Your *heart* knows it.'

Ronnie felt a wave of emotion so strong she had no control of it. It surged in her chest and flooded her body, finally spilling over. Hot tears slid down her face and she fought with her breath to stop them. She mustn't wake her grandmother.

'Water heals,' said the angel. 'Your body is mostly made up of water and you cannot ignore it. It's part of your environment and there is good reason for its presence, but ultimately, you must allow it to surface from within and release it. It is this knowing that brings balance and the healing that's needed. We are here, making ourselves known to you. You are never alone…no one is.'

Ronnie managed a smile through the tears, 'Is this what's meant by the flow?'

'Exactly,' said the angel, 'Immerse yourself in the ebb and flow of the water of life and give up all resistance.'

'I can't swim.'

'Learn! You have a good teacher…' the angel was laughing again, and slowly beginning to fade until the light had dimmed completely.

The room moved into sharper focus and Ronnie was aware of the solidness of it all and the density of the atmosphere.

The temperature had changed again. It was warmer now. And where there had been a brilliant light, there was only a dim and empty space. The being had gone. So this was knowing. Yes it was real and she couldn't ignore it, but what was she supposed to do about it?

The soft rapping on the front door made her jump and she was there in seconds. The sight of Joe on the doorstep with Morrigan in his arms almost made her cry again.

'Hi there,' said Joe, passing the squirming toddler to her, 'Sorry about the delay. We had a bit of a hold-up.'

'What happened?' said Ronnie, kissing her smiling daughter, 'You've been ages!'

'Yeah well, you'll never guess what happened.'

Joe followed her into the kitchen.

'Try me,' laughed Ronnie as she cut slices of cake and piled them onto a plate, 'Not much would surprise me at the moment!'

'Pray tell.'

'I will, but tell me first.'

Joe took off his baseball cap and ran his hands through his hair, 'Well after you went, we bumped into that woman from the garage with her dog – a really nice spaniel – Dilly thought so too, as it happened…' he peered up at her.

'And?'

'Well, I'd kind of forgotten that Dill's in season, Basil being as good as he is, since he had the snip he doesn't take much notice… But the other dog was a bit more interested!'

Ronnie glared at him, 'Are you telling me what I think you're telling me?'

Joe popped a piece of cake into his mouth and nodded.

'Did they get tied up?'

'Oh yeah, in a right knot. Must've been a good half hour we were standing there waiting. You can't separate a pair of dogs once they're tied up like that you know, it's dangerous - you have to wait until it's all over. We had a nice chat anyway, me and Martha... her hubby's got a boat down the marina.'

Ronnie crossed her arms, 'So what are you going to do now? Take Dilly to the vet's?'

'Actually, no. That's a real nice spanner, plus he's a pedigree. A good one too by the look of him!'

'So that means...'

'Dilly's up the duff with a bit of luck,' Joe beamed at her, 'Oh come on Ron, you've got to admit it would be great wouldn't it? Puppies! And nice ones at that... they'll fetch a good price.' He bowed his head and looked up at her.

'I suppose you discussed that with *Martha* while the deed was being done?'

'We did actually, yeah. But it's not just that, think about how much fun it'll be and how Morrigan will love it!'

Puppies, on a boat, with a toddler. Did she even want to imagine it? Was this what the angel meant by *going with the flow*? She looked at Joe - the sparkle in those eyes - why would she want to snuff that light out? She couldn't even if she tried. 'I just don't believe what you're like sometimes, Joe. How do you think we're going to manage? It's not as if there's loads of room and we're prepared or anything is it?'

He grabbed her and wrapped both arms tight around her, burying his face into her hair, 'We've got plenty of time – nine weeks to be exact - besides Ron, sometimes you just have to go where the tide takes you and not worry about it. Maybe it was meant to happen? You can't always make preparations for things, life isn't always like that. Being spontaneous, that's all part of nature Ron, going with the flow is the only way.'

Ronnie managed a smile as her grandmother's voice crackled across the hallway…

'Are you there? Is *anyone* there?'

'Just coming Gran.'

They walked together into the living room to find a grinning Morrigan carefully placing tiny fistfuls of soggy cake on the arm of her great grandmother's chair. The old woman's face was a mixture of shock and amusement at such an awakening.

Joe started to laugh but was quickly stopped by Ronnie digging him in the ribs.

'Bet you weren't expecting more cake quite so soon were you Gran?' said Ronnie, herding the toddler away.

'Who does she belong to? Not yours is she?'

'Yes that's right, Gran. Don't you remember me telling you? You *have* seen her before, you know you have!'

Ronnie hurriedly cleared away the clumps of sodden cake, pushing them into Joe's hands and directing him out to the kitchen.

'Never seen her before in my life,' said the old lady reaching for her frame. 'Now I need the loo. Are you going to stand there like a bloody lemon or help me?'

'How long before your mum gets back?' said Joe in a hushed voice after the toilet operations were over.

'Soon I hope. Honestly, she changes like the wind, my Gran. You should've heard her earlier…such a sweeter old lady you'd be hard pushed to find.'

'I know where I'd like to push her now…off the end of one of those pontoons at the marina.'

Ronnie punched him softly in the side, 'Joe, please don't…she doesn't mean it, really she doesn't. I've always got on fine with her.'

'Yeah, that's because you're more tolerant than most.'

She laughed, 'Certainly more than Mum anyway!'

'No it's more than that Ron, you've got something...you forgive people, that's what you do. It's a gift, something special. *You're* special.'

She looked at him, 'Really? Do you think so? I just do what feels right, what comes natural that's all. I'm just myself.'

He winked at her, 'Glad to hear it. Don't think it'd work like it does for us if you were someone else. There's not many who'd put up with me.'

'Probably not, but I'm getting kind of used to your style and that pirate blood of yours.'

'Oh and you'd be exactly right,' said Joe stroking the silver ring in his ear, 'Never doubt it my good lady. We're a good match you and me!'

'Yes,' she said, placing the Temperance card back in the red pouch, 'And talking of going with the flow, I need to call on your skills remember?
I have to learn to swim.'

11

The Tarts and the Stag Horned God

After trampling through endless tracks of ferny undergrowth and several arguments with bramble bushes, Minerva was ready to stop for refreshments.

'Is there anything in particular you'd like to focus on for a spot of magical work?' said Gerald between mouthfuls of mini-pork pies.

Minerva detected a certain air of superiority. 'Can you pass the brandy when you're ready Isis?' she called across to her friend. 'Such a beautiful spot for a picnic. I would never have imagined a grove of Oak trees in amongst all this lot.'

'It *is* a wood Minerva,' said Isis, passing the bottle.

Don't you start, thought Minerva, shooting her a warning look.

'I thought we'd begin with a tree meditation,' said Gerald polishing off another pork pie. 'Very grounding.'

Minerva narrowed her eyes at him, 'I'm feeling quite grounded at the moment, thank you.'

'And thirsty too, I see.' Gerald smirked at the almost empty beaker in her hand.

'I'm enjoying myself,' said Minerva, 'Or at least I *was*. Correct me if I'm wrong, but I thought the purpose of this trip was to relax and have a bit of fun!'

Gerald glanced sideways at Isis. 'And you would be absolutely right Minerva. The intention has been to give you whatever you need, of course. I just thought a spot of magical working might be in order as *part* of the fun. Nothing serious you understand.'

'No, actually I don't,' said Minerva downing the rest of her drink in one, 'The magical work that I do, I happen to take quite seriously, in fact. And I certainly don't do it for *fun* Gerald as that would suggest dabbling as far as I'm concerned and I do *not* dabble in magic. It's a sacred act for me.'

'Oh I would agree wholeheartedly,' said Gerald, 'It was only something very simple I had in mind...just a small ritual to honour the Wood Spirits and to make the most of the energy for any personal work. But if you'd rather not, that's perfectly fine, we can just enjoy the magic of our surroundings without any of the formalities.'

He removed his jumper, propped it underneath his head and lay back, looking up through the dappled shade to the patches of sky between the tops of the trees and began to hum tunelessly. Minerva cleared her throat and poured another brandy, 'Well, if that's what you had in mind I suppose it might be a good idea.' She paused for a moment, 'Actually there *is* something I have in mind which would benefit from some retrieval magic and it would be helpful to have some additional power.'

Isis coughed loudly as she scrambled to her feet and headed for an opening in the trees, 'Just answering the call of nature...back in a minute.'

'I'm glad you're coming round to a magical way of thinking.' smiled Gerald.

'Oh believe me, it's very much my normal state,' said Minerva, 'But surely... *you* will know how important trust is, especially when it comes to fellow workers. One has to be extremely careful...I hardly know you from Adam. Isis is the only link between us and even so, we haven't known each other long.

'The unknown can certainly be an uncomfortable place for some...' said Gerald.

'Oh *please*, spare me the mystery and intrigue Gerald! I'm afraid it doesn't wash with me. Let's get something straight right now before we proceed any further... I've been a Witch all my life and probably in many others too, I don't need you or anyone else to start Lording it over me, so quit now. It's a pointless exercise.'

She couldn't be sure if it was a shadow or a smirk that came over Gerald's face.

'Understood Minerva. Talking of which, are you sure you're up to the work as *standing* will be required...and you've had a few to put it bluntly.'

'If it's blunt we're talking then your powers of observation would appear to be slightly below par as I've only had two drinks thank you,' snorted Minerva, 'And I suppose the half empty bottle of ginger wine that you've been tucking into doesn't count at all?'

He had the nerve to laugh out loud and she wanted to hit him.

'Touché my Lady! I think it's quite obvious we are magical equals. I too have been a Witch as far back as I remember and beyond, so we have nothing to prove or lose. In fact there is everything to gain...'

'Anything happened yet?' said a red-faced Isis returning from her trip.

'You have,' said Gerald planting a kiss to one side of her hairpiece, 'A joy as always, my love.'

Minerva was quite relieved to feel like a gooseberry again. Three was a far better number for magic anyway, particularly the sort of magic she had in mind. 'Shall we get started then?' she said, glancing at the light through the trees, 'the magic is waiting to happen, I can feel it.'

'Right,' said Gerald, 'Isis, would you mind making up a toast for the Gods – something to eat and drink - and is there anything you need to gather for your work, Minerva?'

'Is there a Willow around here anywhere? I need a branch or at least a piece of one.'

'There's a brook running over there,' Gerald pointed to the edge of the wood, 'and there's a huge one alongside it, you can't miss it.'

'Will bakewell tarts do?' said Isis rummaging through the hamper.

'Very nicely,' said Gerald, 'I'm partial to a nice tart or two.'

Isis and Minerva looked at each other.

'You're treading on dangerous ground, Gerald,' said Minerva, making her way to the brook.

She was glad to have a moment to herself. It was at this hunting and gathering stage when the magic really began to run freely through her veins. Thoughts would pop into her head telling her where to go and she was always drawn to exactly what she needed. It was something she'd learnt to trust implicitly without question. Magic was her greatest friend.

There it was.

The Willow stooped over the brook, its branches combing the water as it trickled along. *It's singing,* thought Minerva with a smile as she got closer and the gurgling got louder. She stopped for a moment, scanning the ground for any fallen branches, which, she noticed, would involve crossing to the other side of the brook over stones of various shapes and sizes covered in moss.

Slimy moss.

She contemplated the unsteadiness of its nature and decided there was nothing else for it but to make a swift attempt to cross. I must bring Morrigan here, she thought, taking a deep breath and picking her way over the slimy stones. Before reaching the other side, she spotted a branch of the perfect size and thought how much more pliant it would be from its time in the water. Instead of waiting until her crossing was complete, she attempted to bend down and pick it up…and down she went. There followed a crashing and splashing of arms and legs and a good deal of swearing…a brief interlude of discord as the sweet gurgling song of the brook turned sour with Minerva's cries.

'Oh for Goddess sake! Bloody *hell,*' she wailed at the Willow, grabbing its trunk with both hands and pulling herself up, 'Is this a joke?'

She could have easily cried but thought better of it. She had work to do, but the physical contact with the tree was something she knew she needed when she felt it charging her with its earthiness. As the current ran around her body, she smiled at the sun on her soaked clothes and breathed in the warm air.

'Okay, okay, I get it,' she whispered, 'Earth, air, fire and water. ..*Yes.* Thank you for the reminder but if you don't mind me saying, perhaps a little more subtlety in future? I *know* you're there, really I do. But I need this magic from you today so please, if you wouldn't mind, may I have a small piece of your good self?'

She looked down at the branch floating between the slimy stones, unattached as it was, but still very much a part of its source and holding the qualities she knew she needed for her spell. The power of the earth was like no other when it came to healing and with its help she'd get back what had gone missing. This wasn't about hoping or even believing. It was about knowing.

Feeling energized by the calming waves flowing through her, Minerva picked up the branch, her spirit lifting as the smooth, damp wood fitted easily into her hand. 'Thank you!' she said to the tree bowing before her and slowly made her way back to the others.

* * *

'There you are!' said Isis, 'You're soaking wet…where have you been Minerva?'

'Where do you think I've been? Following the instructions to find this.' She held up the branch, 'Mission accomplished as you can see.'

'Not without the water spirits claiming you first by the look of it,' said Gerald.

'Are you ready to start?' said Minerva before turning to the Willow, 'If I can just have a few minutes to spend on this then I'll be with you…'

'Don't you want to change out of those things?' asked Isis, looking more concerned than ever, 'I have a spare wrap around skirt, if you like?'

'I'm perfectly fine as I am, thank you Isis,' said Minerva. 'These hot flushes do come in handy sometimes. Any spare bakewell tarts going?'

'May I ask what you're going to do with that?' Gerald pointed to the damp piece of Willow which Minerva was carefully laying on the ground.

'Have you ever made a boomerang?' said Minerva picking off the wet leaves.

'I had one when I was young, but no, I don't think I ever *made* one,' said Gerald narrowing his eyes.

'Don't you make sure the bend is in the middle?' said Isis handing a squashed tart to Minerva.

'Yes, that's right,' said Minerva. 'Not that it matters too much if it doesn't work technically. The important thing is that it will work magically, but I'd like to make it at least *look* like it's a boomerang, if you know what I mean. Symbolism is everything don't you think, Gerald?'

'Absolutely. How are you going to maintain the bend?'

Isis began to fumble furiously with her hair and within seconds, had two elastic bands to hand to Minerva. Gerald watched as the glossy and coppery clump of hair fell to the ground, before hesitating and giving it back to Isis.

'Thank you,' said Isis. 'Do you have a pen knife on you by any chance?'

'Er...no, actually, I don't,' said Gerald, feeling his pockets and looking embarrassed.

'Oh, I know,' said Isis, darting over to the hamper and after another rummage, pulled out a small vegetable knife. 'Perfect. You can make a bit of a dent with this either side of the middle and with a bit of luck—'

' —the bands will have something to keep them in place and we'll have a bend. That's quite genius,' said Minerva, 'Well done. What do you think Gerald? How's that for inspired work? We know how to improvise don't we Isis?'

She held up the Willow, bent and secured with elastic bands, by which time Gerald was busy helping himself to the ginger wine.

'And what about this? said Isis, handing over a bakewell tart.

'Oh yes, an important ingredient without which,' Minerva paused, 'there might not be the desired effect.'

With that, she began to rub the whole of the rather crude looking boomerang with the squashed tart.

Isis glanced at Gerald, who merely shrugged his shoulders, 'And what would that be Minerva?'

'Sugar has profound summoning powers, and therefore it's only common sense to use it in this spell, you see...' said Minerva. 'It's amazing what comes to mind as soon as one tunes into a magical wavelength wouldn't you agree Gerald?'

Minerva carried on rubbing, only looking up when no answer came.

'Oh Gerald's gone to *change,*' said Isis, looking over her shoulder. 'He'll be back soon. He likes to get himself ready, like you do Minerva.'

'I'm pleased to see he takes his magic seriously,' said Minerva, popping the remains of the bakewell tart into her mouth, 'And I'm sorry I misjudged him Isis, it was presumptuous of me. It's the strain of everything at the moment. But today has really helped, I feel a hundred times better already just by being out in this wonderful place with people who...well, *care.* It's the perfect tonic for stress and the strain of my mother at the moment. I have thought at times, that I was a lot closer to the edge than usual. This has brought me back to myself. I feel completely grounded again. Thank you.'

'That's quite all right,' said Isis, 'It's good to see you back to yourself again...and in your *magical* element.'

'Being with the right people makes all the difference, especially when it comes to working magic,' said Minerva, 'And Gerald seems to know what he's doing.'

'Oh yes, I think you'll see that he does.'

Isis continued with the finishing touches by arranging the bakewell tarts and brandy on a wooden bread board. Placing their used beakers beside the food and drink, she tottered over to a patch of grassy ferns with the spare wrap around skirt and laid it neatly on the ground. She knew it would come in handy for something and no circle was complete without an altar of some kind.

Meanwhile, Minerva was busy scribbling on a piece of cardboard - the only writing material she could find - replacing the existing text with her own. Somehow she couldn't quite cover up the words but it would have to do. What counted were her words, not the bakewell or the tart, and she concentrated hard on putting as much feeling into it as she could.

'Right then ladies, are we ready for the off?'

Minerva's renewed state of serenity made it easier to ignore Gerald's bossiness,

however, what she couldn't ignore was what he was wearing.

She'd never liked paisley. It reminded her of her Uncle Frederick who'd spent all his time strutting around in a dressing gown covered in the ghastly pattern. According to Aunt Delilah, who pandered to his every whim, his *smoking jacket* was a symbol of his refined character. Funny how the oddest things could scar a memory for life.

Could Gerald be Uncle Frederick reincarnated?

'I think we're just about done,' said Isis, out of breath. 'What about you Minerva?'

'Yes!' cried Minerva, holding the Willow aloft, 'As ready as I'll ever be...'

It was then she noticed the antlers, perched at a precarious angle on Gerald's head, 'Are they real?' she said.

'They certainly are,' said Gerald puffing out his chest, 'I had them specially mounted onto a headdress for ceremonial purposes. Wonderful aren't they?'

'He's the Stag Horned God, King of the Wildwood.' It wasn't like Isis to interrupt or sound smug, but she managed both which surprised Minerva.

'Yes, I can see that,' said Minerva. 'But aren't they a bit heavy?'

'They're not the easiest or the most comfortable things to have on one's head,' said Gerald, 'Which is why we need to get on with it. Can't keep it up for too long.'

'No, quite,' said Minerva beginning to feel uneasy, 'Lead the way then, Gerald.'

She tried to make eye contact with Isis as they followed him over to the ritual area, but Isis had her head down, deliberately placing her feet where Gerald had left his, while Minerva avoided every invisible footprint she could at the rear of the procession.

To the unknowing, the threesome made a peculiar spectacle: A paisley clad and stag horned Gerald, a star struck Isis with a wobbling bread board of brandy and tarts and a soaked Minerva, clasping a soggy boomerang. Minerva's eyes darted around the grove and she had a sudden desire to make a hasty exit but something was stopping her. She mustn't lose her nerve, it was only a bit of fun in the woods after all. No doubt all would be revealed before long. How right she was, although not quite in the way she may have thought if she'd had the luxury of time to imagine it. But she didn't.

Once all three of them were gathered in the centre of the circle, the pace of events quickened. In one sweeping move, a ripple of paisley and a gasp from Isis, Gerald stood before them, wearing nothing else but a smile. Minerva swallowed and blinked hard, several times. It was all she could do to fix her eyes upon the paisley dressing gown cast aside on the ground inches in front her as Cordelia Nightshade's garden and the life art class flashed across the screen of her mind.

Not knowing what to do next, she quickly averted her eyes to Gerald's headdress as it was the safest place to look and the least embarrassing option give or take a horn or two. And she reluctantly allowed her gaze to slip down to his face as he began to speak...his carefully chosen words booming around the ring of trees.

'Spirits of the Wildwood! We gather in celebration, a union of hearts and minds, in *your* honour, on *this* day. And so, I cast this circle...'

He was not entirely unconvincing and Minerva did her best to stay focused as she turned the boomerang over in her hands and said a few silent words to the Goddess. She would remember why she was here and what she would say when it was her turn to speak. It was important to get these things right, especially at times of reverence, like this. That was providing nothing else got in the way of the magic.

The prickles of a hot flush in its early stages began to creep under her skin and as much as she tried to suppress it, the heat quickly surfaced in its usual, uncontrollable way. She noticed how her hands were sticking to the damp boomerang and thought how sweat and sugar were not the best combination on such a warm day. On any day.

The buzzing didn't bother her at first. There was nothing

like being outside with all of the earth's creatures, and Mother Nature's soundtrack was the perfect accompaniment for any ritual. Gerald continued to call in the quarters and talk to the spirits...hands waving wildly and horns tipping dangerously to one side. And when everything began to wobble Minerva wondered how she was going to manage to retain any sort of composure at all. Keeping her eyes fixed firmly on his tilting horns she held on tight to the hot and sticky boomerang...and her breath.

'...And the spirit of *all* things, every creature of the Great Mother, we welcome you!' Gerald concluded in puffs and pants.

In that moment, Minerva wondered how the power of such authority could be ignored.

'Aaaargh!' cried Gerald.

'What is it?' said Isis, startled out of her trance.

'I've been stung!' Gerald hopped from one leg to the other, clutching his manhood and his horns as they toppled to the ground.

Minerva didn't know whether to laugh or scream.

'Oh dear!' said Isis, flapping like mad, 'Wasps!'

'Bastard, bloody things!' shouted Gerald, doubling up in pain.

Being directly behind him wasn't the best of positions for Minerva. She'd never wished for paisley quite as much as she did in that moment. Looking down at her hand and the buzzing boomerang she flung it outwards as hard as she could in the direction of the surrounding trees. It was the kind of reaction anyone would make under attack from an insect not best known for its friendly behaviour.

But what she didn't realize was that the boomerang would do

exactly what it had been designed to do and return to where it had come from. Lightening reflexes, more by default than design, caused Minerva to duck at just the right moment.

At least for *her*.

Unfortunately, Gerald, in such an uncompromising position, happened to be in the direct line of fire and didn't escape the sticky boomerang's swift return. And of course the wasps, true to form, were first on the scene.

It wasn't a pretty sight.

The wasps were delighted with so much naked flesh on display and sugar so readily available, and who could blame them? Meanwhile, Isis had managed to grab the paisley dressing gown and cover the writhing Gerald while Minerva removed the sugar coated boomerang and hurried over to where she'd found it in the first place. She washed off as much of the sugar as she could by submerging it in the cool water of the brook but could not bring herself to leave it there. How could she do such a thing after it had proved its abilities so well? No, this was a magical tool indeed and it was going back to Crafty Cottage with her, where in private, she would conclude in her own ritual the retrieval of her lost libido. She couldn't think of anything more effective.

The Goddess was definitely good. But poor Gerald wasn't. She wasn't sure he'd deserved to be so cruelly punished for his blatant display of the wild and stag horned God but when it came to magic, one could never be too careful. And for anyone who crossed the boundaries in any way, the Gods had their own ways of dealing with them. It wasn't so difficult to understand when she thought about it. Reverence for the natural world and honouring the Gods was something that was second nature to her, and meeting David had only reaffirmed her beliefs. He may have a different God to believe in but he showed him as much respect as she did her own and together they shared their common belief and love for the sacred and the divine. Suddenly she missed him and wanted to get back. Ronnie had probably had enough of her mother by now.

'Minerva...there you are!' Isis appeared, beetroot faced, almost falling into the water as her arms flapped about her like a windmill.

'I'll be with you in a minute,' said Minerva, holding the boomerang under water. 'Just giving this a final rinse...'

'Oh...' said Isis, 'Do you have anything? *Anything* which will soothe wasp stings? Gerald is covered in them!'

Minerva jumped up, 'Do we have any vinegar?'

'No!'

'What about lemon juice?'

Isis thought for a moment, 'I don't think so...'

'Ice?'

'*No*! What shall we do? He's in a bad way...'

'Is there any swelling in his mouth or throat? Can he swallow? Is he still breathing okay?'

Isis frowned and began to chew her lip, 'Well he's making a lot of noise...'

'Let's get him down here,' said Minerva, marching back in the direction of the grove. 'He needs cooling off...the water will do it.'

Isis didn't say a word but followed Minerva back to the groaning Gerald, hunched on the ground by the hamper. She was alarmed to see a man she'd grown very quickly to look upon as a tower of strength in such a sorry state. Her eyes flitted to the brandy bottle and back to Minerva.

'Come along Gerald!' shouted Minerva. 'Over to the

brook…now!

'What?' bleated Gerald.

'Get up man will you!'

Gerald staggered to a standstill, Isis grabbed the brandy and the pair of them followed a marching Minerva to the brook and the Willow tree. No sooner were they there, Minerva gently pushed the paisley clad Gerald towards the edge of the bubbling water, 'In you go Gerald…lie down and get completely under the water if you can. It will help, really it will.'

Gerald said nothing and practically fell into the water, the dressing gown opening out like a fan around him.

'That's better, isn't it?' said Minerva looking away.

Gerald whimpered as he spread-eagled himself across some rocks and slowly turned over. Minerva spun round to find Isis drinking from the bottle of brandy, 'Pass that over when you're ready,' she said, 'I'm parched.'

'Yes, thirsty work this magical stuff isn't it?'

'It can challenge the best of us at times, Isis.' she said, glancing sideways at the bare skinned Gerald, sprawled over the rocks. 'One never stops learning.'

'You're right, sorts out the men from the boys eh?'

The fiery liquid caught in Minerva's throat, 'Did you really say that?' she gasped, spluttering and coughing while Isis patted hard and fast on her back.

'I did. Am I cruel and heartless?'

'Not at all,' said Minerva. 'Funny how certain things can change our perspective don't you think? Magic works in mysterious and wonderful ways.'

Isis frowned and tilted her head in the direction of the trees and the unmistakable rapping of the Woodpecker, 'It certainly does,' she said with a sigh. 'Nothing will surprise me anymore.'

'Oh really?' said Minerva, catching the floating paisley out of the corner of her eye, 'I wouldn't be quite so sure about that.'

12

Murderous Tendencies

A few days later, Ronnie was drying off in the sun after her first swimming lesson. The low murmur of voices prompted her to open her eyes and she watched as a couple strolling down the pontoon came into view. The shoes gave them away.

Everyone who owned a boat at the marina wore the flat, leather decking shoes in dull and muted tones of ochre and navy or green and beige. The woman's laces were undone, drawing attention to her long, tanned legs and bleached denim shorts. A blonde ponytail bobbed out from a bright red baseball cap sheltering a young but serious face. The older man looked happier, grinning and gesturing with his hands. He wore a red polo shirt strained over a huge belly and dark green shorts, with an air of authority about him. There was something about them which made Ronnie feel uneasy.

She smiled when Joe appeared from inside the boat carrying two mugs, 'There you go, special mermaid tea, just as you like it.'

She laughed, 'I'm not sure I've earned that title yet.'

'Duck to water, literally...' said Joe, glancing up at the approaching couple, 'You'll be swimming the channel in no time.'

'I don't know about that,' she said, following his gaze.

As the two people drew closer the likeness between them became obvious. Now she knew who it was. The father and daughter ambled towards the barge and Ronnie pulled her towel closer and reached for her sunglasses.

'Hi Ronald!' called out Joe. 'Good to see you again.'

He grinned and stepped towards the edge of the deck.

'Joe, hello there!' said the older man. 'Yes, it's been a while. Been overseas for the past few months, I'm allergic to the cold weather as you know.'

He reminded Ronnie of a posh father Christmas, all red and jolly and polite.

'Well you picked the right weather to come back to. We've been looking after that boat of yours, put her in the water yesterday...she's all ready for you. Hello Penny, how's it going?'

She knew that face was familiar. It was Posh Bird, daughter of boat owner.

'Hello Joe,' said Posh Bird, looking slightly ruffled. 'So *this* is where you're living now.'

'Certainly is,' said Joe. 'And you remember Ronnie don't you?'

Without waiting for an answer, he turned to face Ronnie and winked at her, 'We like our new home don't we Ron?'

'We do,' she said with a smile. 'Nothing like being on the water...actually.'

Posh Bird gave one of those smiles that didn't reach her eyes and began to fidget and play with her phone in a dismissive manner. Joe and Ronald exchanged boating talk for a few minutes while the daughter ignored them all. How awful to be so rude, thought Ronnie. Only stupid, posh bitches behaved like that.

'Anyway…must be getting on,' said Ronald beginning to walk away. 'Got a boat to get out on!'

'It's a grand day for it,' said Joe. 'Water's like a millpond…'

'And I thought it was still waters that ran deep,' said Ronnie looking at the boat owner and his daughter as they continued their way along the pontoon. 'All feels a bit *shallow* if you ask me.'

Joe laughed, 'Now, now Ron, sarcasm's the lowest form of wit you know. It doesn't become you.'

'Yeah well…' sighed Ronnie. 'Funny how some people affect you that way isn't it?'

'Only if you let them. You're better than that…' said Joe, tweaking a corner of her towel, 'At least I thought you were!'

She removed her sunglasses slowly and narrowed her eyes at him, 'Honestly Joe, you have to admit, she's an awful snob isn't she? It was as much as she could manage to string a couple of words together.'

'So nothing's really changed there. But I noticed she was giving you the beady green eye though…'

'Really? That must have taken some effort, no wonder she didn't say much.'

'What do you expect? She had the stuffing knocked out of her when you came along didn't she? And now that we're living together…that's really rubbing salt into the wound, right?'

'Are all posh birds like that?'

'How would I know? I only went out with the one and that was enough, thanks.'

'It was for quite a while if I remember rightly'.

'Well, I don't actually recall much of it if you really want to know. You came along and that was it as far as I was concerned, no contest. Now can we talk about something else do you think? Old flames bore the hell out of me.'

He was a charmer all right. It was one of the reasons she'd fallen for him in the first place. But did he mean it? Was he over Posh Bird completely? He was saying all the right things, but then in front of her he would wouldn't he?

She wasn't so sure.

As her mother would say, *time would reveal all.*

* * *

'What the hell is that thing?' mumbled Cybele, pointing to the mantelpiece. Spitting most of a mouthful of porridge out, she ignored it as it dribbled down her chin and onto her clothes.

'What *thing*?' said Minerva, staring at the sticky globules bouncing on the hairs of her mother's chin.

She knew what her mother was pointing at - the boomerang perched rather grandly between two red candles on the mantelpiece had managed to retain its shape despite its unfortunate history - but there was something about not acknowledging the obvious straight away and making her mother work harder for an answer. She knew it was a lowly form of entertainment but found a perverse pleasure in it. When it came to her mother, she couldn't help but take advantage of what little power she had left in a situation she had no control over. It was only natural.

'That bloody thing there..!' spat her mother, red in the face, 'What's a bent up old stick doing in the house?'

'I could ask you the very same same question,' Minerva

mumbled into her coffee.

'What? I can't hear a bloody word you're saying...speak up! You know I'm deaf.'

'I *said* it's a boomerang, made of Willow...' shouted Minerva, 'Can't you tell?'

'I tell you what I *can* tell, you're as mad as ever, always have been a strange one, you. I blame that daft bloody father of yours'. He meddled in magic and all kinds of weird shenanigans. No wonder you turned out the way you did. Silly changeling bitch!'

Minerva dug her nails into her scalp and thought of another use for the boomerang. Willow was the ideal weapon - so *flexible*. Just a quick tug once it was in place around the scraggy neck, that's all it would take.

But what about the body?

It would involve a lot of digging, so earth might not the best choice. A nice pyre perhaps, in the back field... Bonfires were quick, with few left overs. Ash wasn't too much to get rid of was it? She could go down to the beach and scatter them at high tide with a bit of help from a good, south westerly wind. She'd find a dollop of dog poo and throw it in for good measure. So nice to include *all* the elements.

Balance was everything.

'What are you doing that for?' said her mother as Minerva turned the television on, 'You never do that unless I ask you to and even then, you moan about it!'

'Well maybe it just so happens to be the easy option today,' sighed Minerva, a hint of resignation in her voice. 'I don't have the energy to battle with you anymore, mother. And since arguing the toss seems to be one of your favourite pastimes, best that you do it with whatever daft presenter who happens to be on the telly, just like you usually do.'

There was silence from the corner where the old woman hunched over the remains of her porridge. That's shut you up, thought Minerva.

She turned the volume up until it boomed and left the room, leaving her mother glued to the flickering screen in front of her. Funny how something so mundane could have such a magical effect. She hated the television almost as much as she despised her mother. They were welcome to each other.

She found herself wondering if she knew of a dodgy electrician, someone who could fix the insignificant box in the corner of the room with some sort of detonating device, timed to go off when there was no one else in the house or anyway near it…except for her mother. It could be messy though, and of course there was the fire risk, but worth adding to her list all the same. It was true what they said, you had to be very careful what you wished for…it was important to get it right.

Only the right electrician would do.

'Minerva, there you are…I thought you were out.'

She almost jumped out of her skin as she looked up and saw Isis standing in the kitchen, right in front of her.

'Good Lord and Lady, Isis, don't do that to me!' said Minerva clutching her chest, 'Or there's a good chance I could go before she does…and that would not be good on any level, if you know what I mean.'

'No, I don't know what you mean…' said Isis slowly.

She thought Minerva had an odd look about her as she watched her scribbling fiercely on the back of the porridge oats packet. She'd seen that look before, usually when Minerva was under the influence of those hormonal horrors.

'No of course you don't Isis, it wouldn't enter your head

would it?'

'Is it the men-o-whats-it thing again?'

'The what?'

'You know...hormones and all that?'

'You mean that ghastly disease that reigns over my body and washes me up on the shores of insanity on a regular basis? *That thing?*'

'Yes, that...thing.'

'Although it can't be ruled out Isis, and thanks for the reminder, I think at the present moment you'll find the problem is in there,' Minerva pointed her pen at the living room, 'Strangely enough the two *things* are similar in nature, both appearing to cause a considerable amount of imbalance and the arising of certain feelings.'

'What kinds of feelings?' said Isis, trying to ignore the cold shiver running down her spine.

Minerva held up the porridge oats packet. Isis didn't like the gleam in her eye, it reminded her of the wicked queen in Sleeping Beauty. Her eyes darted over the spidery scrawl:

1. Earth - Bury – garden/back field

2. Air - Suffocate – pillow/bean bag

3. Fire - Burn – unfortunate television explosion

4. Water - Drown – bath/pond

When? Where and How?

'You will notice there's a word left out...' said Minerva in a business-like manner.

'What?'

'Exactly. Well spotted,' said Minerva, 'And as you can see it's all quite self explanatory really. Method needs no other explanation does it? You can't beat a clear description, and as you know, I believe in keeping things simple.'

'There is another word you've left out,' said Isis, scanning the soggy cardboard.

Minerva thought for a moment, 'No, you've got me there Isis. What?'

'Why.'

'Don't be awkward,' sighed Minerva.

'I'm not,' said Isis, 'That's it.'

'What?'

'No, not that. *Why!*'

Minerva wanted to hit her, 'If you're not careful Isis, you'll end up on this damn list too,' she paused for a moment, 'Oh I see...*Why.* Do you really need to ask? Is it so unfathomable?'

'No not really. I think I'm beginning to see, it must be hard, yes, I can see that.'

'Good,' said Minerva, 'Because I really don't have the energy to explain anymore. I think it's safe to say, murder is on the cards as well as a morning tipple.'

Isis couldn't find anything safe to think or say about murder at all as she watched Minerva pour the brandy into two glasses before shuffling the Tarot cards.

'There we are,' said Minerva with great conviction, propping up a card against the brandy bottle, 'I knew it.'

Isis peered closely at the image, 'High Priestess...What's there to know about her?'

'Good question,' said Minerva. 'The High Priestess knows it all you see, she possesses all the wisdom there is - she doesn't need to look outside of herself at all, doesn't have to. It's all on the inside. Wisdom from beyond the veil says it all don't you think?' She pointed to the pomegranate covered veil behind the mysterious female figure.

'So what does that mean?' said Isis, enjoying the warm

brandy creeping into her stomach.

'It's obvious. It can only mean one thing...pomegranate is the fruit of the dead.'

Isis spluttered on a mouthful of drink and began to choke as Minerva thumped her hard on the back, almost knocking her over. After much slapping and spitting there was an eerie silence in the kitchen while the two women looked at each other.

'You wouldn't would you?' croaked Isis rubbing her throat, 'I mean, you couldn't...it wouldn't be right Minerva.'

'Do you think what I'm going through is *right?*'
She spoke through gritted teeth and her eyes narrowed into two dark slits under her blood red fringe.

'She's your *mother*'.

'She's making my life hell. And a quick trip to heaven makes perfect sense for the both of us. She's almost there anyway isn't she? Ninety one for Goddess sake! The deed, if I made it quick would make it heavenly for both of us do you see?'

'What about David?' said Isis holding out her empty glass.

'What's he got to do with it?' said Minerva, reaching for the brandy bottle as some noisy crows outside caught her attention.

'He's a vicar and he's your boyfriend!'
The desperation in her friend's voice was lost on Minerva who was already lost in a world of her own. Murder and madness went hand in hand after all.

'I don't see what that's got to do with this situation Isis, really I don't. As far as I'm concerned it would be doing everyone a favour...putting the pair of us out of our misery if you like.'

Isis glared at Minerva, speechless.

'All I'm doing, or thinking about doing, is accelerating the process that's all.'

'Please, Minerva,' pleaded Isis, glancing nervously at the High Priestess. 'Search within yourself. *Think about it.*'

'Oh I'm doing all that,' said Minerva, 'And it's really rather wonderful because the answers seem to be coming straight away…look!'

She nodded to the kitchen window where a deafening sound was coming from outside. It sounded like cats fighting but Lucifer was nowhere to be seen, only a flock of birds circling in the sky above Mr. Morris on the drive.

'See what I mean?' said Minerva, 'Crows Isis! The Goddess doesn't talk plainer than that does she?'

'You mean it's a sign? I don't really see…"

'And an obvious one I'd say…' said Minerva pouring herself another drink. 'A flock of birds is a flock of birds, yes, but when it's *crows*! It's a murder isn't it? Never underestimate the power of Nature's oracle, Isis…it speaks to us all the time. We have only to observe and understand it, that's all.'

Isis was too busy with her own observations to think about what the birds were saying. She had no doubt Minerva was being serious, she was sure of it, but whether her calm exterior was enough to carry out the dreaded deed she was speaking about Isis couldn't be sure. Hopefully, it was just another one of Minerva's melodramatic episodes.

'The W.I.' said Isis, slowly.

'What..?' said Minerva still staring at the crows circling overhead, '…are you talking about?'

'It's what *they'll* be talking about which I thought might be of interest.'

'And what might that be?' said Minerva, impatience creeping back into her voice. 'What wondrous original recipe or never been done before knitting pattern is up for discussion this month? Don't tell me they've finally come to their senses and are replacing the acoustic version of the national anthem with the Sex Pistols rendition. I can just hear that blaring out in the village hall…a refreshing change don't you think?'

'It's a talk on Witchcraft believe it or not,' said Isis. 'I heard them talking about it in the shop earlier.'

'Are you sure?' said Minerva, tearing herself away from the window, 'I find it hard to believe the Jam and Jerusalem brigade would even entertain the idea of something as edgy as the Craft. Paper doilies, crotchet hooks and coach trip knickers aside…it's not your *average* craft by any means is it?'

'Well no, but I'm only going on what I overheard in the shop. Maybe David could enlighten us on the subject. They do still have their meetings in the room at the back of the church don't they?'

'As far as I know, yes,' said Minerva, 'Who's giving the talk? I can't imagine it would be anyone other than a history buff can you?'

Isis shrugged, 'I've told you all I know. It's tomorrow night so why don't we go along and find out? It might help to take your mind off things.'

'You might be right there,' said Minerva, placing the porridge packet face down on the table, 'Perhaps a night out is just what I need to take the pressure off.'

Isis nodded a bit too enthusiastically, causing her hairpiece to topple forwards onto her forehead. With the brandy slowing her reflexes she ignored the expression on Minerva's face and continued, 'Quite right,' she said, 'Do you think you could temper all murderous tendencies and put any such plans on hold until afterwards?'

'I will certainly try,' said Minerva. 'But don't ask me to swear on my mother's life, that would be too much to ask.'

13

Dead Man Talking

David wasn't used to interruptions. Taking up residence at the vicarage in Cragwell on Sea had very quickly accustomed him to the quietness and slower place of village life. The transition from Ireland to England had been far from smooth but he preferred to leave all that in the past now. His position in the village parish suited him just fine and was more than any batchelor or man of the cloth could hope for, especially after the kind of life he'd had.

The banging continued until he left the comfort of his armchair to investigate. 'Isis!' he opened the door wide to let her in, 'It's not every day of the week the vicarage gets a hammering...you'd better come in!'

'David I'm sorry to be a bother,' said Isis, wringing her hands, 'But it's Minerva...'

David pointed the way to the living room where he directed Isis to sit down on the huge beige sofa. He watched her as she grappled with the lop-sided clump of hair, pushing it back to the top of her head while she fought to catch her breath.

'Take your time Isis' he said, 'And when you're ready, please tell me whatever is the matter.'

Isis looked up at the angels on the ceiling and managed a watery smile.

'You've just come from Crafty Cottage then I gather?' he said, 'And a late morning tipple no less! Glad to see you've been enjoying each other's company!'

'Yes, I mean no,' said Isis. 'No, it didn't start like that. The brandy helped actually, it was the only thing that did.'

'Isis,' said David firmly, 'Is Minerva okay?'

Isis let out a heavy sigh, 'I'm not entirely sure to be honest, David. It's her mother, you know how it is!'

'I do, yes,' he said. 'Trying at the best of times, especially for Minerva. But she's coping mostly, wouldn't you say?'

'No, I wouldn't say…at all, actually,' said Isis. 'She's on the edge if you ask me and it's very worrying. I've never seen her like it before.'

'What do you mean exactly?'

'She's making plans…'

'What kind of plans?'

Isis couldn't look at him and began to play with the bangle on her arm, 'Plans that involve her mother and certain means of disposal afterwards.'

Isis glanced nervously at David who didn't even flinch.

'This is sounding quite sinister, Isis. Are you sure?' said David. 'Would you like a strong coffee?'

'That's because it is, and yes I am and yes please, I will,' said Isis, concentrating hard and forcing herself to look at him.

By the time David returned with the coffee she was sweating profusely.

'Do you have a drop of anything stronger by any chance?' she asked, her eyes flitting back and forth from the window to

David.

'Isis, is that absolutely necessary? What I mean is, perhaps you've...'

'Had enough?'

There was a certain high pitched tone to her voice.

'I know how persuasive Minerva can be.'

He smiled and passed her a mug of very dark, strong smelling liquid.

'You don't believe me.'

'Isis, it's not that I don't believe you...I am trying to understand what's going on here,' said David. 'But you must admit, it does sound quite fantastic and as much as I am familiar with Minerva and her foibles shall we say, I think disposing of her mother might be a step too far in this case, don't you?'

'You mean I've gone a step too far in my assumption or Minerva's plans have gone a step too far?'

'Well...'

Isis looked at his feet. They were bare and smooth and very clean and his crucifix glinted in the sunlight. He's just like Jesus, she thought. 'Look David,' she said in a much lower tone, 'I have just spent the last hour or so with Minerva. She is not herself, and all I will say is, no matter what you think you know, murder is very much on her mind. Now I don't know about you but I don't think it's something anyone can ignore. She is my friend and I'm worried about her and I'm worried about her mother and I'm worried about what will happen if nobody does anything to stop it!'

David raised his hand, 'All right Isis, I will go round there and see how the land lies if that makes you feel any better.'

'It would, yes...thank you,' she said. 'Minerva listens to you, normally. Although this isn't really a normal situation is it?'

'I agree, but let's see how it unfolds,' said David. 'It's certainly worth a try.'

'I can't help but feel guilty,' said Isis chewing her lip and nudging her hairpiece back into place. 'I wouldn't usually go behind anyone's back, especially Minerva's!'

'There's no need, Isis,' said David. 'You're only doing what you think is right and that's all anyone can do. And it's exactly what a good friend would do.'

'You think so? I feel like a very bad one at the moment.'

'Not at all,' said David. 'Minerva is fortunate to have you, really she is.'

Isis suddenly felt better. Perhaps the hand of God had something to do with it, or the coffee. Whatever it was, she was grateful for heavenly helpers and feeling sober again.

* * *

Ronnie had a feeling she couldn't shake off. Lurking in the corners of her mind and spreading to her body was a sinking in the pit of her stomach like a lead weight. It woke her up in the middle of the night, and lulled by the swell of the water, she was reluctant to leave the warmth of the bed and Joe beside her. She wanted to stay there but something would not let her be, so she got up as quietly as she could and left Joe and Morrigan sleeping. She passed the dogs on her way to the tiny kitchen and patted Dill who woke up immediately while Basil remained in a deep slumber beside her. 'Hey Dilly,' she whispered, 'Not long now eh? They'll soon be the patter of tiny paws!' She put her hand to the warm, furry belly and was sure she could feel some kind of movement from it. Dill craned her neck and sniffed at the stroking hand. 'How many d'ya reckon then girl? I guess we'll have to wait and see.'

Birth was a magical thing and so closely partnered with death when she thought about it. It was hard to separate the two when she'd experienced them so close together. Morrigan's entry into the world could never make up for Bob's sad exit but now she viewed it differently. And now that she'd seen Bob and felt him, she knew he wasn't gone completely...only from this world.

As she made some tea the cool air from the water brushed past her, or at least that's what she thought. When the shiver ran up her legs and spine, the tingling was too much to ignore. And when it met with the feeling in her stomach, she knew. Someone was there, she just didn't know who. Swallowing hard and trying not to panic, she made her way slowly to the small living area between the bedroom and the kitchen. Dill was right behind her, slumping at her feet as she sat down carefully on the small sofa. She was glad of the company, and although she sensed they were not alone, the dog showed no awareness of any danger which was a comfort.

As Ronnie sipped the hot tea the feeling became stronger. She heard a shuffling in the corner by the wood burner, and the familiar smell of sweet tobacco filled the air reminding her of Ropey. He'd smoked that stuff, when he was alive.

'It's all right Ron, I don't mean no harm.'

A voice from the dimly lit corner forced her to look up and hold her breath. There, in full physical form sat a man on the old armchair with the white cat on his lap, looking very much at home.

'Ropey is that you?' Ronnie struggled to keep her voice as low as possible.

'That's right Ron, just me and the cat, just checking up on

you that's all...'

'Oh,' she whispered, 'Keeping an eye on us are you?'

'I am,' he said, 'I care what happens here. This is my boat remember. Just me and the cat were the only ones for a long time.'

She could hear the cat purring as he stroked it. 'And how are we doing?' she asked. 'Up to standard or not?'

The familiar laugh was unmistakable, 'I should think so,' he chuckled, 'But you've got your hands full. What with your little one, the dogs and more on the way...'

'Yes I know,' sighed Ronnie, 'It's a squeeze and it's going to get tighter.'

'But you'll manage just fine,' he said, 'You have a good captain on board.'

She smiled, 'You're right, Joe looks after us very well.'

'And so he should,' said Ropey, puffing on his pipe, 'Taught him all I know.'

She looked at the figure in the chair. He looked just like any other person and as physical as anybody alive. The smoke billowed around him and the cat purred on his lap. She could see, hear and smell... all the evidence of the physical senses was right there in front of her. How was any of it real?

'I know what you're thinking,' he said, 'It's a strange one isn't it? This being dead business. I'm still getting my head around it myself. Never mind them *folks* – there's now't as queer as being dead!' He chuckled and coughed.

'So how come I can see you if you're dead?' said Ronnie. 'Can anyone else see you too, or is it just me?'

'That's a good question,' said Ropey grasping his stubbly chin. 'I've never really felt like coming back till now if I'm honest so I can't answer without trying it out on anyone else. But I knew it would be night time and that you'd all be sleeping and that's why I came. Didn't want to disturb anyone you see? I always was a thoughtful chap if you remember rightly.' He winked at her.

'I do indeed, Ropey,' she grinned at him. 'The perfect gentleman as always. But why me do you think? Why are all these weird things happening to me?'

'You're talking about recently?' said Ropey, 'When you fell into the water after you spotted the cat…?'

'Yes! So you know about that. Looks like I was right about the cat,' she said slowly. 'Joe didn't believe me.'

'No, but apart from what you'd told him he didn't have any reason to did he? That's because he had every reason not to believe it. He knew she was dead you see. He'd been told remember?'

'Yes I know,' said Ronnie, 'But what about what happened after that? My experience. Do you know about that?'

'I do, yes' nodded Ropey. 'Don't ask me how. Just because I'm dead doesn't mean I know everything and how it all works, because I don't. It's all a bit of a mystery if you ask me. But I'll tell you one thing young lady, that particular day you had a very near miss – or shall we say the kiss of death more like?' He stopped to chuckle again, 'Whatever it was, it was with the other side as I'm sure you're aware of. Not a completely unpleasant experience though was it?'

'No it wasn't, it was like a dream,' said Ronnie. 'I heard angels and I saw Bob, my horse…'

'I know you did. And you travelled like you used to with him, just like old friends do. He was just as real as the cat here, and me talking to you. How can that be? What's the reason for it? I'll tell you Rhiannon without telling you much at all if you can understand an old man gabbling on, and a dead one at that - it's because there's something you can do, something you can give to others. Exactly what that is I'm not entirely sure, as I'm not rightly informed on these matters. But I do know that this world of the living as we call it, is not all there is. There is more, as you've seen, you've been there...had a glimpse of it if you like. And that was to show you, to let you know that when you think it's all over, it bloody well isn't. I'm living proof after all!'

He chuckled once more and Ronnie found herself chuckling along with him. She wanted to ask him more questions. But the laughter began to fade as Ropey disappeared altogether. The old man and his cat were gone, like the feeling in the pit of her stomach. She was getting used to the language.

14

Jam and Jerusalem

Isis stood in the doorway, pressing her silky handbag close to her heaving chest, 'Can we wait for Gerald?' she said. 'He said he'd like to come if you don't mind?'

'No, I don't mind,' said Minerva staring at the bright green bag. 'I'm getting used to playing gooseberry, but we're already late. Don't want to miss those opening bars of the mighty Jerusalem now do we?'

'I suppose not.'

Minerva grabbed her purple poncho and favourite green velvet hat before turning to Isis, 'Hang on a minute Isis, he *can't* come! It's the W.I. remember? Women only if I'm not mistaken, although one could be forgiven for assuming *weird individuals* might be a more accurate description, especially with Tilda Herd on the door.'

'Tilda Herd,' said Isis, frowning, 'Isn't she a he?'

'Exactly,' said Minerva. 'And regardless of whatever operation he or she may have had, there is no denying he or she has the physique of a man. Built like a bulldozer wouldn't you say?'

'Yes, I would say. The legs give it away if you ask me.'

'Absolutely. Those massive calves would be much better hidden under a decent length maxi skirt instead of those ridiculous just below the knee numbers. But I have to say it's the face that does it for me. How can you not recognize a masculine jaw line so perfectly square as Tilda's? I have to wonder why these men go through with such an operation on their lower realms when they could clearly do with a head transplant as well.'

'Yes,' sighed Isis, 'You have to feel sorry for them don't you? It can't be easy.'

'And it's certainly not easy for the rest of us either,' said Minerva. 'Keeping a straight face when the builder who repaired your roof and guttering not so long ago now struts about in a skirt and slingbacks is a tough one - painful in fact. The last time I bumped into him outside the shop I spent the entire time working my pelvic floor muscles so hard to prevent leakage it not only left me acutely embarrassed but also wondering if I was the one with problem and not him…or her.'

'What do you mean?' said Isis moving closer to Minerva.

'What I mean Isis, is that problems breed problems.'

'Ah yes, I see…' said Isis, her eyes widening like saucers, 'You mean like attracting like?'

Minerva thought for a moment, 'In a way, yes, we're all infectious energetically, aren't we?'

'I'd never thought of it like that.'

Isis jumped out of her skin when the doorbell rang. That will teach her to stand right by the front door, thought Minerva.

'Good evening ladies!'

Gerald stood on the doorstep with outstretched arms and

Isis fell into them, reminding Minerva of a Venus flytrap.

'Well it is for us Gerald, but sadly not for you,' said Minerva trying not to sound smug. 'Isis forgot to mention one minor detail on the Witchcraft talk tonight…it's at the Women's Institute!'

Isis pulled away from Gerald's arms, 'How silly of me,' she mumbled into her hands, 'I'm so sorry Gerald. It does seem terribly unfair!'

'No men allowed I'm afraid,' interrupted Minerva. 'Not unless you're Tilda Herd, formerly known as Terry, who's gender, as far as we're concerned, remains debatable.'

'And what's he or she doing there?' asked Gerald looking alarmed.

'He or she will be on the door as usual, I presume…and there'll be no questions asked because he or she will be wearing a skirt, bright orange lipstick and a big square grin.'

'Does he or she join in with Jerusalem?' said Isis, 'Because that will sound a bit off won't it?'

'Now you have me quivering in anticipation,' said Minerva, 'But you're quite right, even without the talk, it's worth going along just to hear the dulcet baritones of Tilda's singing. Oh and not forgetting the national anthem at the end…' she clapped her hands together, 'An evening of entertainment lies ahead, I can see it now, Isis. Let's get going! Are you walking back as far as the church with us Gerald or would you like to keep my mother company for a couple of hours? She's sleeping at the moment in the front room and will probably drift in and out of consciousness for the rest of the evening. That's pretty much all I can guarantee I'm afraid, otherwise you take your chances on mood, language and sound effects…all of which are subject to change at any time and usually when least expected.'

Gerald cleared his throat and gently coaxed Isis out of the front door, 'I think you've made my mind up, thank you Minerva. Your wonderful prediction of your mother's unpredictability leaves me no choice but to escort you lovely ladies to the church door and to he or she who guards it. At least I hope to get a glimpse of this infamous person you have so eloquently described. Do you think if I put on a skirt and lipstick, I'd get away with it?'

Minerva narrowed her eyes at him while Isis gasped in horror, 'Oh Gerald, no, please don't!' she cried, 'One Tilda Herd is more than enough and besides, you're far too much of a man to even think about it.'

Minerva felt slightly uncomfortable as she shut the front door and followed the giggling pair down the road, before calling out ahead, 'How are those stings coming along Gerald? Healed up yet have they?'

After a long enough pause Gerald answered in a sobering voice, 'Healing nicely, thank you for asking Minerva. The combination of brook and brandy sorted them out a treat.'

'Yes, I've always found to achieve maximum healing benefits it helps to work on both the inside and out,' said Minerva, quickening her pace.

* * *

The trio made their way through the church gate where they were met by a fourth person making his way to the entrance of the fine building.

'Good evening people!'

The lilting Irish tones and gleaming smile seared through Minerva like a hot knife and for a fleeting moment she thought about the boomerang.

'David, what are you doing here?'

'I was just opening up for the ladies.'

Minerva shot Isis a sideways glance, 'Are you sure about that?'

Isis gasped, her wide eyes darting backwards and forwards between them.

'I have these to prove it Minerva,' said David, holding up a set of keys.

'Yes I know,' said Minerva, 'But can you prove that inside those sacred walls, they are all ladies?'

Isis let out a high squeak, while Gerald chuckled.

David grinned at her, 'Enough of the cryptic and mysterious, Minerva, what do you mean?'

'That's what I mean, over there!' she hissed loudly, gesturing towards the shaft of light escaping from the partly opened church door.

David raised an eyebrow and followed her gaze, 'I'm not with you at all I'm afraid, can you enlighten me in any way perhaps?'

As if in answer to his question a tall figure in silhouette came into view, blocking the light completely.

'There,' hissed Minerva into the palm of her hand, 'Over there, look, in the doorway!'

'You mean Tilda?' David's voice dropped to a whisper too, 'I think you'll find she's one of the ladies, yes.'

The patronizing tone was not lost on Minerva. David of all people wouldn't normally take that attitude. But then, these were not normal circumstances by any stretch of the imagination. She'd forgive him.

'Well, my eyes and ears tell me otherwise. It's quite obvious in my book,' she said.

'Shall we go in?' said Isis, peeling herself away from Gerald, 'It'll be starting soon.'

'Yes all right,' huffed Minerva, 'I suppose we'd better, before the trumpet sounds and Jerusalem reigns down upon us!'

There was a short silence and a shuffling of feet.

'Care for a drink at the Druid, David?' said Gerald brightly, patting Isis gently on the bottom.

Minerva gave him a dark look.

'I would indeed, thank you Gerald, sounds like a marvellous idea. Enjoy your evening ladies!' called back David as the two couples parted company.

Minerva hurried to the half open church door and peered around it with great caution.

'Why hello Minerva,' said a gravelly, baritone voice, 'What brings you here tonight? Don't tell me you've finally succumbed to the wonders of the W.I.'

Minerva couldn't help but stare at the tall and cumbersome frame of Tilda Herd bent double behind a small table in front of her.

'Not ready to sign up for the Jam and Jerusalem membership quite yet, thank you Tilda,' said Minerva grappling with her bag, 'Not sure I'll ever be a lady, unlike your good self of course.'

'We've come for the talk!' blurted out Isis, sidling up beside Minerva, 'Who's doing it Tilda, do you know?'

'A very learned looking lady, by the name of Brenda Squash I believe,' Tilda was reading off a piece of paper in front of her, 'A historian of all things!'

'Can't say I've heard the name,' said Minerva, 'But that would explain why, as I don't normally mix with the scholarly types. Squash you say? You look a bit squashed yourself behind there if you don't mind me saying so, Tilda.'

'You're right there Minerva,' said Tilda with a big square grin, 'I'm not best equipped for the reception job I must admit.'

'I couldn't agree with you more,' said Minerva, uncertain of what exactly she or he *was* equipped for.

'To be fair though Tilda,' said Isis, 'Those silly tables are unusually small aren't they? Not built for the larger frame at all.'

'I shall manage,' said Tilda with an air of confidence and glancing over to the back of the room, 'If you want to get a seat, I'd go in if I were you.'

Quite relieved that Tilda wasn't her, Minerva smiled sweetly and led the way into the church hall. As they meandered their way through the groups of tables and chairs, an assortment of faces looked up at the wandering pair. A low mumbling filtered from each table rising and falling like a tide as Minerva and Isis offered humble grins and nods in their direction.

'You can sit here!' squawked a woman with orange hair and bright red cheeks.

'It's Old Ma Flapper,' whispered Minerva under her breath, 'Taking us under her wing.'

'Oh,' said Isis, hesitating, 'Shall we…or not?'

'Plenty of room here,' said the woman, patting the empty chairs, 'Sit yourselves down me dears'.'

She beamed a toothy grin at them, which blended in nicely with her heaving bosom and ruddy complexion. Minerva thanked her and steered Isis to sit down.

'Not seen you two here before,' said the orange woman, 'I'm Patty Flap.'

Minerva wasn't sure if it was a question or a statement and before she had a chance to answer a well spoken voice struck up at the back of the room. It came from a woman with a shock of white, bobbed hair sitting next to a much smaller woman with curly, dark grey hair. They looked particularly official, shuffling large bits of paper, the grey curls and the white bob meeting at frequent intervals as they talked between them. And yet it soon became apparent they were not as well organized as they could have been as they continued to discuss any forthcoming announcements at length between themselves. Passing a large radio microphone back and forth between them, they thanked, introduced and announced all kinds of people - who's existence they were unsure of as well as half-planned outings they weren't sure would go ahead - to a baffled looking audience.

Minerva shifted uneasily in her set and cast a beady eye around the room at the assortment of women. They were a diverse bunch, gathered in groups of four and five, some in electric buggies, some leaning on walking sticks, but all of them facing the two leaders at the back.

'And so now for Jerusalem!' proclaimed the woman with the straight white bob.

Isis began to fidget while Minerva froze. It was an awkward moment before the whole room burst into song with not an instrument or a piece of music in sight. The dark grey curly woman beamed her way through each verse while the straight white bob sang with less gusto as both chests worked in tandem as the musical crescendo rose and fell with each chorus. Minerva daren't look at Isis, fixing her eyes instead on the two women and mimed her way through the whole affair.

'You can smile while you sing you know!' said the dark grey curly woman afterwards to the audience, 'It doesn't cost anything!'

Minerva and Isis smiled politely in return and Minerva remembered why she'd never been comfortable with institutions or conforming to any set of rules or worse still a belief system that was completely unnatural. It was a herd thing, a following the masses thing and she could never do that, had never done it and would *still* never do it. Buttoning her lips together she stiffened like a rock on the hard chair, grew taller and stared at the wall behind the straight and curly pair while the boring announcements continued to drone on.

Just off to the side of them sat a fidgeting woman in front of a large screen with an overhead projector. She must be the historian, thought Minerva. Yes, those glasses, the slightly dishevelled, fuzzy hair escaping at odd angles from a tired looking bun, almost smartly dressed in a black, mid-length dress with horizontal stripes, a jacket with the sleeves too short and pointy low heeled shoes with scuffed toes; she definitely looked like a history buff. Not quite fitting in was something Minerva could definitely empathize with as she found herself warming to the woman who looked as awkward as Minerva felt.

But, the all important question...was she a Witch?

Minerva scrutinized her immediate surroundings of table and over-head projector and noticed the untidiness of it all (like the woman's appearance) amidst an assortment of haphazardly piled books. She made a mental note to look at those later. The benefit of the doubt was something Minerva didn't give many people but she would, in the historian's case, give it to her. The subject matter at least, deserved a fair trial.

While the two grey mares droned on, the fuzzy haired historian fiddled with a handbag which looked liked it had far too much in it and chewed a pen she didn't write with. Finally,

Brenda Squash was given a grand introduction, gingerly taking the radio microphone as it was passed eagerly to her and apologising when it proceeded to cut out.

Minerva leaned across to Isis and whispered into her hair-piece, 'It's a sign.'

'Of what?'

'Electrics don't just cut out for no reason, Isis.'

'But isn't it battery operated?'

'Never mind that, the point is, Isis, things are happening... or not, in this case. Do you see?'

'I think so.'

Heads turned in unison and the pair found a room full of eyes gawping at them.

'Tell me more, later.' whispered Isis to the floor.

Minerva resumed her upright position at the same time the microphone resumed its volume, blasting poor Patty Flap, who was desperate to hear the conversation between Minerva and Isis. The look of shock on her face turned her ruddy cheeks redder while she clucked loudly and jolted back into her seat.

All eyes turned to Brenda Squash once more as the ghostly font of *Witchcraft in the 16th Century*, clicked onto the screen behind her and a voice piped up, 'Well I never...how's she doing that then?'

The historian assumed an immediate air of importance and smiled, 'Ah,' she said, 'That's modern technology for you...no magic there I'm afraid!'

Enough was enough as far as Minerva was concerned.

A true Witch does not make a mockery of magic. It was like biting the hand that feeds you. After that it was downhill from thereon in and she cringed when the Squash woman mentioned the hangings as 'gruesome and awful' in a melodramatic voice.

'She's getting on my nerves,' said Minerva, crossing her arms.

'Really?' said Isis.

'Did we bring the brandy? I'm not sure a tea or a coffee will hit the spot.'

'Well I didn't bring any.'

Minerva looked around to see Patty Flap swigging from a silver hip flask.

'Care for a drop of the hard stuff?' she said to Minerva with a wink.

'Thanks very much,' said Minerva.

And so continued the patronizing quips from the scruffy historian punctuated by the odd interruption from the odd members of the audience. And when it was finally over Minerva was feeling far less irritated by the performers after warming up nicely from the contents of Patty Flap's hip flask. It was a welcome break. As were the plate of French Fancies, delivered to the table by a small, elderly lady with a distinct shudder.

'No homemade Victoria sponge?' said Minerva with a dead pan look.

'Minerva!' blurted out Isis, 'Who's patronizing now?'

'What dear?' said the tiny figure, in between shudders.

'Thank you Audrey,' said Patty Flap, grabbing one.

Isis followed suit while Minerva reluctantly reached out and took one for herself.

'How much longer?' she asked, scanning the room and popping a whole French Fancy into her mouth.

'I don't think we'll get out until after the national anthem,' said Isis.

Minerva sighed, 'I'm not sure I can take much more of this.'

Jumping out of her chair, she proceeded to make her way out with Isis springing into action behind her. They weaved their way back through the groups of tables while the women huddled around them looked up with vague expressions as the two friends made for the exit. The two grey mares looked up in unison from the top table before muttering something to each other. In the meantime, the fuzzy haired historian fiddled with her projector while Patty Flap grappled with a second French Fancy.

No one really cared they were going, apart from Tilda Herd who piped up as they passed her at the door, 'Leaving so soon you two?'

'I don't know how you do it Tilda, really I don't,' said Minerva leaning across the narrow table, 'Did you know that the opposite of courage is not cowardice but something else completely?'

'No?' said Tilda, leaning back, 'What is it then?'

'Conformity,' said Minerva, straightening up and pausing for a moment, 'That's what it is… it is the most suffocating thing to befall the mind of man…or woman come to that.'

Tilda looked at Isis who was looking at Minerva who was standing with her chest puffed out like a pigeon and fanning herself with one of the leaflets.

'I'm not sure I…'

'No of course you don't,' said Minerva.

Isis pulled the purple poncho towards the door, 'Come on Minerva, if we want to catch the Druid before closing time…' It was a desperate attempt not to sound as desperate as she felt.

'Goodnight ladies!' said Tilda, 'Perhaps we'll see you next month!'

'I don't think so Tilda,' said Minerva, 'Now excuse me while

I return to the land of the living and breathing once more!'

Out she strutted with Isis scurrying after, leaving Tilda Herd behind the church doors shuffling piles of leaflets and wondering about the meaning of conformity.

'You've planted a seed,' said Isis catching up with the marching Minerva.

Minerva spun around in mid-stride, 'What?'

'Conformity,' said Isis, 'To Tilda of all people! Although, it might well confuse him or her...'

'Not a bit Isis,' spat Minerva, 'He or she is already dutifully molded into a W.I. clone, that much is obvious. Nothing will move him or her, not while those over-sized feet are firmly fixed beneath the under-sized table.'

'That's conforming then is it?' said Isis.

'That,' said Minerva, stopping at the door of the Old Druid, 'is the ultimate form of it, yes. Joining these institutions and mass minded groups may be a source of comfort to those who do it - it's perfectly natural to want to identify with others who are like minded - but to never break away from the herd? Tilda is certainly living up to her name don't you think?'

Isis stood speechless while Minerva, tossing her red mane back, pranced through the pub door chanting, 'And personally, I can't think of anything worse.'

15

The Magic of Nature

The passing of time brings all kinds of wonders. And whether we know it or not, Mother Nature is the great decider and always right. On the houseboat this particular warm and sticky night, Ronnie was up with one very pregnant and restless dog and only the inky sky for company. She'd left Joe and Morrigan slumbering peacefully in the comfort of their beds when Dill's panting and pacing around became too obvious to ignore. After following the dog onto the small deck where she obviously wanted to be, she sat quietly with her in the cool night air. The water was calm and the sky, crystal clear with a sprinkling of stars. There was an air of deep tranquility and Ronnie sank into it while stroking the broad and silky space above Dill's eyes...preparing herself for what was coming next.

Should she wake Joe?

Not yet perhaps. How long this kind of event would last was up to Mother Nature and her wisdom. She remembered watching a foal come into the world at the stables one night with her mother. They'd waited patiently with Gail, owner of the mare and the livery yard where she kept Bob, and it had turned into an evening vigil complete with flasks of hot chocolate, sausage rolls and sherbert lemons. Her mother and Gail had talked continuously into the small hours while Ronnie watched for the emergence of new life, certain it was going to come when no-one was looking. She never took her eyes off the restless mare who circled round the box, laying down and getting up again at frequent intervals throughout the whole affair. And when the foal finally arrived, it plopped out so quickly while all three were dozing that they almost missed the magical moment. Ronnie remembered it like yesterday, stubbornly hanging onto the memory of her previous horsey life with Bob. How could she forget?

Dill was showing the same nesting behaviour of the mare, craning her head round to her tail, her sides heaving with short, shallow breaths. Looking dazed and bewildered, she seemed unaffected by the lull of the boat's gentle support - and distracted by the waves of pain she couldn't control - sought Ronnie's hand with her nose. It was hot and dry.

Ronnie didn't hear the padding of bare feet creeping up behind her, 'Looks like something's happening then?' whispered Joe, yawning.

Ronnie jumped, 'Jesus! Where did you come from?!'

'The land of dreams,' he chuckled, 'But I had a feeling when I crashed out earlier that tonight might be the night...how's she doing?'

Ronnie continued to stroke Dill's ears, 'All right so far.'

'Shouldn't we take her inside where the whelping box is?'

'Why? She wants to be outside, it's natural for animals.'

'On this hard old floor?' said Joe. 'It might be different if we were in a wood or a field or something with a softer landing pad. I didn't spend hours making that thing for nothing!'

Ronnie got up slowly, 'Come on girl,' she said, but Dill wouldn't move. 'You can't force her to be somewhere she doesn't want to be Joe!'

Joe disappeared inside and after a lot of shuffling the whelping box appeared sideways through the narrow double doors, with Joe's feet poking out underneath.

'If Mohammed won't come to the mountain...' he puffed and put the box down precariously. 'Newspaper Ron, we need lots of it.'

'What about towels? I have a pile ready.'

'Paper's best to start with, we can get rid of it afterwards. Here Dill...' he called to his dog, who scrambled up awkwardly to join him.

They watched as she spun around in circles, tearing the neatly laid newspaper into shreds. Round and round she went, possessed by the urgent call of nature.

'Animal instinct is pretty amazing don't you think?' said Joe putting his arm around Ronnie.

She nodded as they drifted into their roles of silent witnesses, an occasional sigh punctuated by Dill's heavy panting.

* * *

Birth in the wild is a private and intimate affair between mother and offspring and left to run its course includes pain and a lot of hard work...the kind of work which requires the utmost focus and concentration. Dill was not interested in an audience.

Joe ran a hand through his hair, 'It's not called labour for nothing is it?

Ronnie found herself praying to the Gods and willing the dog through her struggle as the minutes turned to hours and nerves turned from doubts of the unknown to wonder of what was to come.

They drifted in and out of what seemed like endless silence.

'Is there anything else we can do?' whispered Ronnie.

'No Ron, just wait, that's all,' said Joe. 'She's doing just fine...'

'But how will we know if anything's wrong?'

'There won't be. She's young and fit and handling it all good...not much longer now.'

Ronnie was reassured by Joe's confidence and right on cue, Dill responded by standing, her whole body tensing up like a scared cat. Craning her head round, she raised her tail high just as something appeared under it. The first pup.

As the tiny creature plopped down, Joe helped to wipe away the bloody membrane from its body while Dill cleared up urgently behind him.

'What shall I do?' said Ronnie, feeling suddenly helpless.

'Get that other cardboard box and put the pups in there until she's done.'

'Are you sure it's okay to separate them?'

'Yes, it won't be for long. Keep them cosy until there's enough of them to keep each other warm.'

Ronnie did as she was told and they worked in tandem with Dill as she produced one pup after another, sometimes ten and twenty minutes apart. The dawn lit up the sky as the longest break between births heralded the new day. Clearing up more bloody slime and newspaper, Ronnie looked anxiously at Dill, 'Is she done?'

'Looks like it doesn't it?' said Joe nodding at Dill's sunken belly. 'Let's put the pups in with her now. She's looking more settled.'

One by one, the velvety, mole-like creatures joined their mother and took up greedily what was on offer while Dill continued to clean up the new arrivals.

'Good work Dilly.' Joe spoke in hushed tones to the busy, new mum, 'All done now girl?'

With a slow beating of her tail she carried on with her new brood and just as Ronnie was about to suggest a coffee to celebrate - Dill shot up from the box and began to crane and heave once more. And with the familiar lift and sideways tilt of the tail it looked like she wasn't done yet.

'A late arrival!' said Joe. 'Blimey, must've been a good hour since the last one at least...'

'Will it be all right?' said Ronnie, chewing her lip.

'Hopefully so,' said Joe peering closer at Dill's tail, 'But no wonder it's taken its time...it's breech.'

'What?!'

'Keep calm, Ron, it'll be fine.'

She didn't say a word and watched him with the straining dog, wondering how he knew what to do. Maybe it was being so close to nature and out in the elements so much that gave him the natural instinct to empathize so keenly with animals and people. Her mother would certainly say it was a magician at work. Minutes passed into what seemed like hours. Ronnie couldn't watch but stared out at the river, diving into its calm waters to soothe her nerves.

'There we are...' said Joe, eventually wiping the last pup over. 'He's a big one, no wonder he got stuck!'

Ronnie turned and touched his arm, 'You're a wonder.'

'Keeping calm is the main thing Ron, nature takes care of the rest, one way or another. Hey, have we got a surprise for

Morrigan when she wakes up to this little lot!'

Ronnie smiled as she put the kettle on. The magic of nature was an awesome thing and the arrival of any newborn was one of life's miracles; sharing it with Joe made it all the more magical.

She watched the early morning sun dappling the water and felt a warm feeling of contentment, like a hug from Mother Nature herself. She spent a silent moment of gratitude in thanks to Freya and the boat spirits and breathed in the peace and tranquility of a new day….until her phone rang loudly and repeatedly, breaking the spell.

Only one person would ring her so early.

* * *

'Thank the Goddess you're here darling,' panted Minerva as she opened the door, 'I don't know what else to do! I can't wake her up!'

Ronnie pushed past her mother and walked slowly into the front room filled with the familiar scent of lavender and eucalyptus burning in the corner. In the same corner was her grandmother in the same chair she always sat in but something was different about her. A stillness.

'Gran?'

Her voice cut through the silence as she approached the bent over figure of her grandmother, huddled in the corner with only the flickering flame of the oil burner for company. As she got closer, she noticed the faintest sound of shallow breathing and the subtle rising and falling of bony shoulders hidden in the folds of a dressing gown much too big for such a tiny body.

But it was a body that was alive. Just.

Ronnie turned to her mother, 'How long has she been like this?'

'Hours, I think.'

'What do you mean, you think?'

'Well, she was like it when I got home last night. I'd only been out for a few hours,' Minerva glanced across at the cuckoo clock on the wall, perched at an odd angle next to the Green Man. 'I never leave her usually, you know that! I didn't think it would do any harm...I was only down the road for Goddess sake! And she was fine when I left, well enough to drink a large gin, anyway.'

Minerva stared at her daughter and pointed to the empty glass by the armchair.

'Gran, Gran...' Ronnie gently pushed the frail and bent up figure which yielded by tilting further towards the glass and began to convulse without any sound. It was most odd.

'Have you had any sleep Mum?'

'No, I daren't. Do you think we should call the doctor or something?'

'Don't you bloody dare!'

The words were barely decipherable between the sudden coughing and spluttering.

'Mother, you're alive...I thought you'd gone.'

'Disappointed are you?! I didn't go anywhere...but you did, you stupid bitch! Left me here to fester...alone!'

Minerva looked uneasily at Ronnie and back again at the armchair, 'You were perfectly all right when I brought you this.'

She grabbed the empty gin glass and held it up in front of her mother's face.

After another bout of coughing the old woman turned her head towards her daughter and fought for what little breath she had left, 'Mother's ruin eh? You'd know all about that...'

'Mum, go to bed,' said Ronnie quickly, 'I can look after Gran...go on!'

Minerva went without a word or a backward glance. Sleep seemed a very good idea and besides, she was past caring anymore. Guilt was a burden she was tired of carrying.

All those years of not meeting her mother's expectations, never quite coming up to standard. Never being enough. Although, she reminded herself, guilt in the face of such ingratitude was not such a heavy load and she felt it slip as the memories returned with every harsh word that had ever passed her mother's lips. If she doesn't go of her own accord I shall finish her off myself, she thought, as she climbed the stairs slowly and deliberately. By the time she'd reached the top, a plan had formed.

But she wouldn't tell anyone.

Revenge was best sought as a solitary pursuit.

* * *

'Are you going to read to me?'

'I can do that if you want Gran, yes.'

Ronnie grabbed the angel book and began to read in the quietest of voices. She didn't want to disturb her mother further although so far she seemed to have made a pretty good job of it on her own. She'd never seen her so stressed out, even when she'd found her doing a handstand by the greenhouse in the middle of winter with a spider right under her nose.

No, this was much worse. There was an eerie kind of feel to the whole situation now that Ronnie didn't trust and it scared her. Mum wasn't herself.

She just needed some time off that was all.

'It's my last day on earth you know.'

Her grandmother's weak voice made her smile and Ronnie sighed, 'Okay Gran, then we'd better get on with the story then before you pop off.'

'I think they're here.'

'Who?'

'Those angels…look.'

Ronnie studied her grandmother's tiny frame in the chair, bent up and folded like one of those wooden toys she remembered making at school once, with a faraway look in her eyes.

'What can you see Gran?'

'I'm not sure, but it's big…'

She gasped and covered her mouth with her hand. Ronnie followed her gaze and at first couldn't see anything, but sat quietly holding her grandmother's other hand - the faint trace of a pulse beating beneath the paper thin skin. There it was again, a sensation familiar to her now. The rush of energy filled her body as it fizzed up through her legs and along her spine. And slowly a faint light appeared - she could just make it out – there in front of them. The more she stared, the stronger the light became, filling the space and becoming bigger until the whole room was illuminated not only with light but something else. But she couldn't make out what it was.

'It's true isn't it?' whispered her grandmother.

Ronnie wasn't sure whether she was speaking to her or the light.

'What is, Gran?'

'I'm tired you know…never felt so tired. You've come for me at last…about bloody time.'

As if in answer to her question, the light beamed brighter,

glowing and pulsing with energy. Ronnie saw an image forming in the brightness, the shimmering of great wings…the unmistakable figure of an angel.

'Gran, it's all right,' said Ronnie squeezing the tiny bird-like hand.

'Oh I know that, I'm not scared at all. Lovely isn't it? And the singing, I never heard anything like it…never in my whole life.'

The light continued to flood the room as the image became clearer. Ronnie had never seen anything like it either, but the sound was familiar. That day in the water. The voices. The singing.

Ronnie felt her voice break, 'A heavenly choir just for you Gran…'

She felt a weak squeeze, 'I'm glad you're here Rhiannon, can you see the colours?'

'Yes I can. There's a rainbow right here in the room.'

The light contained all the colours she'd ever imagined and glowed around the figure in a way Ronnie had only ever seen in a painting or a church.

Was it really happening?

'I can assure you it is.'

The great being was smiling at them both and she felt something warm embracing her…every part of her body becoming lighter.

'You're not taking me too are you?'
She hardly recognized her own voice.

The angel laughed and she didn't know what to make of it. All she could feel was the beating of her heart pushing hard against her chest.

'No need to worry, dear Soul, there is nothing to fear. You

stand at the bridge, between the worlds, but you will not be travelling any further. All is well.'

'Easy for you to say that,' said Ronnie taking some deep breaths, 'Standing there larger than life!'

She looked at her grandmother who was smiling like a child at the figure in front of her. Not a bit of her seemed scared - in fact she looked more peaceful than ever - although her breath was shallow and fading. How strange it was, thought Ronnie, the less life there was in her grandmother, the more contented she looked. Suddenly feeling helpless, she touched a bony shoulder, 'Gran,' she called softly, 'Are you okay? Can I get you anything? A drink, some water?'

'Drop of gin would be nice.'

The words were barely audible and Ronnie shot out to the kitchen where for a split second she wondered about calling her mother. No, she wouldn't. Sometimes life dictates what's best just by the way things go and this was going fine without her mother. Why change that?

She placed the glass into the tiny hand, closing her own fingers around the swollen knuckles and gently lifted both up to her grandmother's dry lips, parched by the life leaving her frail body.

'Take it easy Gran,' she said casting a nervous glance towards the angel.

After much coughing and spluttering, her grandmother managed to get some of the drink down but it took all her energy and she fell back into the chair, still transfixed on the being of light in front of them. Not knowing what else to do, Ronnie dipped her finger in the gin and ran it around her grandmother's lips.

'Good girl,' murmured the old woman, 'You always were a

good girl...'

Ronnie caught a choking breath, feeling the tears pricking the back of her eyes, 'Don't Gran, please...'

The light seemed to get brighter as her grandmother looked up and managed a weak smile while the angel looked on. Ronnie watched as the light flooded over and through them. She knew her grandmother could feel it and was being drawn towards it. She saw her sigh as the light merged with the music of the spheres and called her home.

She had never known the power of such peace except for her time in the water. Breathing in deeply and closing her eyes, she remembered what the angel said...and there she was, standing at the bridge...waving goodbye to her grandmother one last time.

16

Mr. Morris and the Mushrooms

Minerva stared at the coffin shaped basket so beautifully made. Willow was such a good choice of course, flexible in every way...but not in any way like the person it carried. Her mother had been the most stubborn and rigid character, all the things Willow wasn't. How strange then, that for her final journey in this world she was to be carried off in something that was totally opposite to her own nature. It was almost as if the Goddess was putting things right, here at the end of one journey, in preparation for the next. How very considerate of her, thought Minerva, riddled with contempt for her undeserving mother.

Silently she thanked the Goddess for her good timing. For removing the trappings of dutiful responsibility and the ill perceived debt she owed the very person who had always behaved so horridly towards her. What a strange upbringing she'd had in her wretched company, for all those years. Oh yes, she knew the feeling of being dragged up all right. But now she could lay it to rest with the person responsible for all those early years of misery.

How much lighter she felt. How liberating it was to know that never again would she have to answer to or be there for the one person who had never really been there for her at all. She was free at last.

'Are you ready Minerva?'

David's hushed, dulcet tones shone through the darkness of her thoughts.

'Oh yes, completely. Never been more ready for anything.'

He put his hand very gently on her back, 'Just a minor hiccup though...had a call from the undertakers. There's a problem with the main car, the one which was going to take us to the field of rest. Tilda's been working on it all morning, but unfortunately, can't fix it.'

'What do you mean he can't fix it...I mean, *she* can't fix it? Argh! This is what happens when you mess around with nature!'

David was quiet, which Minerva found maddening, 'Mechanics are not really my forté. All I know is it won't start and doesn't look like it will anytime soon I'm afraid, not today anyway.'

'So how do we transport this—' she nodded to the coffin, '—this thing and my mother to her final destination? A wing and a prayer I suppose?'

'How about Mr. Morris?' said David, 'My car's not big enough, but your's is an estate...'

'Morris Traveller if you don't mind,' said Minerva, squaring her shoulders, 'With all the original wood still intact to prove it.'

'Yes of course,' said David. 'However, it might just do for the job.'

Minerva glared at David in silence for a moment. 'The job?

You're suggesting we use Mr. Morris as a funeral car?'

Minerva looked at the Willow basket covered with white lilies and lavender, 'Will it fit?'

'Well I'm sure we can make it fit,' said David clasping his dark, goatee chin and pacing around the basket. 'Willow is very bendy isn't it? And of course, Mr. Morris with those rear doors will work a treat. I'm sure they will accommodate anything that doesn't quite fit if it comes to it.'

'Doesn't quite fit? You mean if push comes to shove, which is highly likely, it will just have to hang out the back like some cast off from a rag and bone cart!'

'I don't really see that we have much of a choice in the matter, do you?'

Minerva was too busy sizing up the basket to notice David wrestling with his dog collar. 'Well I'm glad you're so sure of yourself,' she said, folding her arms. 'Oh David how could this happen? I swear it's my mother behind all this, trust her to have the last laugh!'

'I don't know about behind it, she's very much inside it as far as I'm aware,' said David managing a weak smile. 'But laughing about it is not a bad thing Minerva, in spite of the circumstances.'

'Well I can assure you,' replied Minerva in a high pitched voice, 'laughing is the last thing I feel like doing at a time like this!'

'Minerva, we'll have to buckle down and just get on with it I'm afraid,' said David. 'We have a solution to our problem with your Mr. Morris...' he looked at his watch, 'It's almost time, the site is booked for 11.30. We don't want to keep the rest of the party waiting do we?'

'You make it sound like some sort of celebration!' she whined,

'I can't get my head around it at all.'

'It's perfectly normal to have all kinds of mixed feelings, especially in this case,' said David before quickly adding, 'Or in your case, to be precise.'

'That's exactly it isn't it? You think I'm a basket case?' said Minerva shooting a sideways glance at the Willow coffin.

'This is getting ridiculous,' said David before marching out of the room and marching back in again with one brandy bottle and two glasses. 'I think this might be the answer, for now anyway,' he said, pouring out a large shot into each glass.

'Who's driving?' said Minerva, looking sheepish.

'I am,' announced David, carefully placing his empty glass down. 'It's only down the road and through the village after all. You'll be better off in the back with your mother and making sure the basket stays secure.'

'I'm having trouble holding myself together,' she snapped, 'Without the added responsibility of holding onto my mother in Mr. Morris of all things. I can't believe I'm putting him through this!'

David sighed heavily, pouring another double into Minerva's empty glass and passing it to her in silence. He did seem to have an uncanny knack of knowing the right thing to do at the right time and she admired him for that. It was quite impossible not to find his cool exterior in handling these delicate matters extremely attractive. She stared at the basket with her mother on the inside and the Willow on the outside and felt a stirring in her lower abdomen.

Could the boomerang magic be working at last?

'So....' he began with an expectant look in her direction, 'Can I ask yet again...are you ready now for this final journey of your mother's? I have a service to provide and a duty to perform in case you'd forgotten, Minerva.'

'As ready as I'll ever be, I suppose,' said Minerva downing her drink.

David clapped his hands together softly, 'Good, we will make a start then. But first to get this into Mr. Morris,' he said, nodding at the basket.

Minerva looked back and forth between David, the Willow basket and the door, 'I'll fetch the keys...' she said, before scurrying out of the room.

* * *

It was definitely one of the least common funerals David had been involved in. He'd never had to transport a coffin before, especially in a vehicle like a Morris Traveller; but then he'd never known anyone like Minerva who owned one.

It was just as well he was armed with the strength to face these tough challenges in life – or death in this particular case. And when such a thing presented itself on a very windy day in June, it was more than enough to test one such as David, who was blessed with one of heaven's greatest gifts: a calm and steady temperament.

The weather, he observed, was not calm and steady but the rain would almost certainly hold off as it often did with a strong sea breeze. However, this didn't help matters when it came to securing the Willow basket and its various ornamental toppings into Mr. Morris. The wind insisted on scattering the lilies and lavender across the front garden of Crafty Cottage as they carried the coffin to the car. And this was no mean feat in itself; especially with the less than steadier natured Minerva despite the amount of brandy she'd consumed.

'Oh David, the lilies and the lavender, look!'

'Minerva, will you please just concentrate on the task in hand,' said David, walking backwards with great care, 'We can pick those up once we've got this in the car!'

'Typical don't you think? The elements out in force like this? It's my mother you know...she always did like to make things difficult for everyone. Or do you think it's the hand of God?'

'What?' said David, edging the coffin into the back of Mr. Morris, 'Look where you're going Minerva!'

After much bustling and jostling, the basket slid uneasily into the car just short of all the way, with the end jutting out over the wooden bar of the boot.

'Just as I thought,' said David stroking his chin with one hand and pulling out a bungee strap from his pocket with the other. He proceeded to secure the basket as best he could to the car by wrapping the elastic and hook around the gaping doors as many times as possible. Meanwhile, a wind blown and wide eyed Minerva was desperately running in all directions to recover the flying lilies and lavender, strewn across the path and catching in the unforgiving holly and rose bushes.

It didn't end there of course, as David hurried round to the driver's door and tried to start up the car without much success.

'What,' he cried, 'in heaven's name is wrong with this thing?!'

Minerva didn't know whether to be shocked or amused by David's cool and calm exterior slipping before her very eyes.

'You haven't sung to him, that's what's wrong! You need to chant the Mr. Morris spell!'

'Oh I see,' said David, not seeing at all. 'Clearly, I don't have the magic touch. Would you mind instructing me on the finer points required to start it...or him...up?'

Still outside the car, Minerva signalled for David to wind

down the driver's window, which due to its poor condition was not the smoothest of operations and took up quite some time. Eventually, after much jerking and shuddering, Minerva was able to lean in and sing to the steering wheel, dashboard and ignition in succession - David wasn't sure which - but sing she did, at full volume to the car:

'Hail Mr Morris! You must start...Bless your engine, bless your heart!'

Over and over again she chanted, and nodding to David to turn the keys once more, Mr Morris - accompanied by the traditional coughing and spluttering – came to life.

'See I told you,' beamed Minerva through the window.

'Well done, now you'd better get in,' said David, wiping the sweat off his forehead.

'You need to get out first. The passenger door's jammed!' she shouted, running to keep up.

Without saying a word, David slammed on the brakes and jumped out, promptly bumping into Minerva, who clambered across to the passenger seat in a stunned silence.

'Dare I ask again,' said David, throwing himself back into the driving seat, 'Are we ready now for the off…finally? Have you got everything you need?'

No sooner had he realized the error of such a question and before Minerva had a chance to answer, Mr Morris kangaroo hopped into action and chugged off into the village. Such a timely departure could only be heaven sent.

Nothing was stopping them now.

* * *

'Gerald, shouldn't you be putting some clothes on? We need

to be at the Summerlands field by 11.30.' Isis called over the top of the midsummer edition of Cobwebs and Cauldrons, her eyes fixed firmly on the menu page.

The naked Gerald stretched lazily in the sun and looked up at the sky, 'Looks like we're in for a breezy afternoon if those clouds are anything to go by.'

'It's wonderful that you can sense what's going to happen before it does,' sighed Isis.

'It's not so difficult and certainly not a magical act,' said Gerald, walking into the conservatory. 'People nowadays are just too damn lazy to use their own senses. They'd much sooner goggle it or get some app to tell them what's happening rather than work it out for themselves!'

'Google,' said Isis behind the magazine.

'What was that?' said Gerald, batting the pages down with a bare arm.

Isis jumped back, her gaze fixed on Gerald's face, 'It's *google,* not goggle...'

'Clearly I'm stuck in the old ways!'

'I wouldn't say that at all. You've got a mobile phone haven't you?'

'A very basic one. And it does everything I want it to so why would I want one of those all singing and all dancing contraptions? They're the demons of this age of technology....addling our brains and keeping us static while we gather pounds and turn goggle eyed!'

'Yes...' said Isis, beginning to fidget, 'You're absolutely right of course. There's something to be said for upholding the old ways. After all, it's perfectly natural isn't it? Connecting to nature, like you do.'

'It's quite simply just staying in tune with Mother Earth, Isis.'

She loved the way he finished her sentences for her. They were like two fish swimming on the same tide. Her eyes couldn't help themselves but roam over his body. Every muscle seemed to stand out and his golden skin glowed like Apollo's.

He began to gesture wildly, 'Our untamed nature is who we really are after all, before the chains of modernity shackled themselves to those weak enough to believe they could not break free of them! We can cast off anything that binds us, at anytime, but we must be willing to do it!'

His bronzed body gyrated and swayed before her and Isis was becoming breathless, 'Do you have anything cold?'

Gerald stood like a statue and thought for a moment, 'You mean a drink?'

'Yes,' said Isis fanning herself furiously with the Solstice Salad double page spread. 'I could do with one, I'm a bit hot.'

Gerald smiled and kissed her sweating forehead, 'I do hope I haven't caused you to overheat, my darling. Can I get you some tea? It will cool you down.'

'I'm fine, really I am, but yes, that would be nice, thank you,' said Isis, absently wiping her face with the edge of the tablecloth. 'But it's quite all right Gerald, I can make it. You go and put some clothes on.'

She smiled at him as he turned and paraded out of the room like a golden stallion and she felt herself burning up under her thin top. It reminded her of what Minerva had told her about the colour orange…something about the sex chakra and the Stag Horned God. Feeling for the orange crystal in her pocket, she thought how the spell at Beltane seemed to be working far better than she had ever imagined it would. Gerald was magic personified and now they were together, she was almost beginning to think she deserved it, just like Minerva said.

Shaking herself from her daydream and remembering how thirsty she was, she proceeded out to Gerald's kitchen to make the tea. It was a magical haven of a room, full of jars with all kinds of potions and charms in bottles and bunches of dried herbs tied with green gardening string. She savoured the sight and the smells and hummed to herself as she gathered the old navy tea pot and mugs onto a tray and reached for one of the many jars of home-grown herbal teas and added what looked like the perfect mixture to the steaming pot. She inhaled deeply and smiled.

It smelt wonderful.

'Was it your Grandmother's?' said Isis, watching Gerald pouring out the tea with great care; each movement perfectly timed.

'Indeed it was, she loved this old pot,' said Gerald, looking fondly at the cracked and faded rose painted on the side. 'She used to read the leaves afterwards and always very accurate too. I do miss the old girl.'

Just at that moment, the large picture behind them crashed to the floor causing Isis to jump out of her seat.

'Oh my word! What was that?

She looked at Gerald who was smiling broadly.

'It's only Grandmother,' he laughed, 'just dropping in to say hello!'

Bending over to pick up the picture, Gerald held it in front of him and slotted the frame and the smiling face of the old lady back together with the greatest of care.

'Just dropping in you say?'

'She does it all the time. Nothing to worry about. You get used to it, especially when it's been happening all your life.'

'Has it really?' said Isis finishing her tea, 'You mean this sort of thing happens all the time?'

'Yes of course it does,' his voice was calm, 'Why wouldn't it? The other world is only a thought away after all and they're always on the look-out to let us know they're around. And more often than not we miss the signs because they are too subtle for us to notice.'

'I wouldn't call that subtle at all,' said Isis.

Watching him return the picture frame back to its rightful place, she noticed how the muscles in his back stood out beneath the golden skin.

'Can I have another cup please?' she said, feeling the sweat begin to trickle down her spine.

'I think she approves of you, in fact I know she does,' said Gerald, pouring some more tea and handing it to her.

'I see,' said Isis, 'Well I'm glad about that then.'

He felt for her hand which was sweating profusely, and squeezed it, 'It's all perfectly natural Isis...you'll get used to it.'

She coughed, 'I do hope you're right, Gerald, but at the the moment these *magical* ways of yours seem quite strange to me. But yes, I suppose in time, I will see it all as naturally as you do. It's quite a gift isn't it? Minerva has it too.'

'We all have it in varying degrees Isis...but the Witch, there's no doubt about it, is blessed with a definite magical perspective. A knowing.'

'Yes,' said Isis dreamily, 'I think I'm beginning to see that...'

'Are you all right?'

'Oh I'm very all right,' said Isis, 'I believe you've worked your magic on me, as usual Gerald.'

She collapsed into a fit of giggles.

'Isis,' said Gerald quite sternly, lifting the lid off the pot, 'What tea did you put in here?'

'The stuff in the jar…' she giggled.

'What jar was that? On the shelf or in the cupboard?'

Isis looked at him blankly and shrugged her shoulders as he tasted the tea for the first time from his own cup, 'Oh great Gods…it's the magic stuff!'

'Very magical yes,' said Isis leaning towards him. 'How could anything to do with you not be magical? You are the magic man!'

'Isis,' said Gerald sternly, 'You don't understand. The tea in this pot is my magic mushroom tea. It's not your normal tea by any stretch of the imagination and it's potent, extremely potent! How many cups have you had?'

Isis picked up her cup and peered into it, studying the contents. 'Well it's all gone…and look Gerald, it's moving. The bottom is moving….coming alive!'

'Isis, look…it's nothing to worry about, it'll pass in time.'

He looked nervously at the clock on the wall, 'The funeral,' he said to himself before turning to Isis, 'We have a funeral to go to and you have just had two cups of mushroom tea.'

'And very nice tea it is,' giggled Isis, still peering into the bottom of her cup, 'I think your grandmother's still here Gerald…'

'What, in the cup? Can you see her?'

'I can see lots of things! The leaves are talking to me!'

Gerald rolled his eyes, peeled the cup from her grasp and stood up, 'Isis, you're right, my grandmother is very much here, of course she is. But the fact of the matter is we need to be going out now, we have a funeral to go to. Minerva's mother's funeral do you remember?'

Isis froze and stared at the picture on the wall, 'But no one really dies do they? Your grandmother is very much alive you know...I can hear her!'

'That's truly wonderful Isis. And yes, of course she is, I know that and I'm glad. What's she saying?'

'She's saying you need to get some clothes on and get going and you must take your drum because the spirits are waiting for Cybele and you must beat her over the head. Oh! That doesn't sound very nice does it?'

'It's not head, it's hedge!' said Gerald, 'Beat her *over the hedge*...yes, she loved to hedge ride. She means give Cybele a good sending off into the Otherworld. She's really getting through to you Isis.'

Isis was animated and buzzing. Raw, life force energy pulsed through her veins and the voices of the ancestors called to her beyond the edges of time...she could hear the echo of their laughter.

'I feel so alive Gerald!'

She began to dance. To whirl and swirl like a dervish with such abandon, Gerald was mesmerized. It would be easy to immerse himself in the magic of it all but now was not the time. He had to get the Summerlands field and Cybele's funeral...and knew better than to ignore his grandmother.

He'd live to regret it otherwise.

17

Scarecrows or Corpses?

The wind was relentless, which was a good thing in David's mind, as it carried Mr. Morris along quite effortlessly. But no matter how hard he tried, he could not shut the driver's window which meant a noisy journey through the village as the funeral car rattled its way along.

David glanced nervously at the rear view mirror for a glimpse of the coffin which was still there, thank God. And the hastily rescued lilies and lavender danced merrily on top of the Willow basket to the tune of a well worn suspension. These old cars had a lot to answer for.

'Isn't he a dream?' said Minerva, caressing the wooden dashboard. 'Under the circumstances, I think the walnut goes rather well with the Willow wouldn't you say?'

'You mean your mother?' said David, checking the mirror again.

'Yes,' said Minerva, 'She would have been pleased with the combination. We used to have a walnut tree in the back garden when I was a girl, in fact the yard would be littered with them. But she loved to pickle them, and do everything possible you could think of doing with a walnut… funny the things you remember isn't it?'

'Yes it is,' said David. 'Could you just lean back and hold onto your mother, she's slipping around and I don't want to damage her any more than I can help it. This wind is stronger than I thought!'

'I'll try my best' said Minerva, undoing a frayed and very slack, seat belt.

'You're good at that,' said David, patting her knee and smiling at the mirror. 'You're going to have to turn around and get on your knees though, so you can hold her down with both hands.'

'Oh good Goddess really?' said Minerva, struggling to get into position.

'We just have to make the best of it,' shouted David above the wailing wind and rattling window. 'Oh look' he pointed to the church green as they approached it, 'I'd forgotten about the scarecrows!'

'What scarecrows?' called Minerva from the back.

'It's the scarecrow festival remember?'

He'd never heard of anything like it in his home country. But he'd come to realize the village of Cragwell was unique and strangely charming in his short time here so far. Two years was not a long time to be anywhere, but long enough to know that in the rural and remote areas of the planet, the echoes of the past remained. The old pagan traditions still ran beneath the modern fabric of rural life and the villagers here certainly seemed to get into the spirit of it as scarecrows of all shapes and sizes loomed everywhere. They were in front gardens, on driveways and up telegraph poles in every guise you could think of. Last year there'd been a black Elvis in a turquoise one-piece suit, and every year the churchyard put on a fine display of an old fashioned wedding.

'Oh the wedding party!' laughed Minerva, 'I love them don't you? They seem to get more glamorous each year…the bridesmaids are new and the chimney sweep and look… there's you David!'

He slowed down as they approached the church and craned his neck out of the window to get a better view of himself. The vicar in the group was clutching an old bible to his chest and the straw was poking up through the slightly askew dog collar.

'Good lord,' said David, absently touching his pony tail, 'He's even got hair like mine, would you believe it? Who made them? They're very good aren't they?"

'Tilda does them I think,' said Minerva, 'With such a knack for dressing up, it's hardly surprising is it?'

'I suppose you have a point there,' said David. 'What a wonderful spectacle.'

Old cars like Mr. Morris require high levels of concentration to keep them out of trouble, although distractions can make it unavoidable. Unfortunately, potholes are common in rural areas but with most of his attention on the village green and the wedding party, David missed the large one by the church. Mr. Morris didn't, however, and with a shriek and a shudder came to a deadening halt just outside the village shop.

Such an impact was not enough to secure the bungee cord holding the vehicle's rear doors together, causing it to hit the postman, who luckily for him, happened to be another scarecrow in disguise. Speed brings the quickest of changes and as the combined forces of a high travelling wind and bungee cord knocked his hat into the air, the rear doors burst open to release the coffin in clumsy and unceremonious fashion onto the road.

It was an ugly scene and one which David regretted instantly but was helpless to reverse as the series of unfortunate events unfolded before him. Minerva had never been a good diver, but the situation called for lightning reflexes, and her brave attempt to follow the Willow basket as it flew out of the back of Mr. Morris was admirable. Sadly, it was not enough to stop the coffin escaping from Mr. Morris or her mother escaping from the coffin.

David was dumbstruck - and not knowing whether to laugh or cry - managed a combination of both as Minerva's mother landed with a thud on the uneven road followed in quick succession by her daughter. It crossed his mind briefly how odd it was to see the dead and the living in such close proximity as he feverishly searched for his crucifix. He was getting very hot under his dog collar.

'Oh my Goddess…' screamed Minerva. 'David! Oh dearest Gods, Mother!'

Minerva's cries were carried by the wind and the postman's hat as it sailed through the air and down the road. After pushing with all his might against the stubborn driver's door, David tumbled out and into the road amidst the lilies and the lavender as Minerva and her mother piled awkwardly on top of each other. Things were getting messy.

'Get off, get off her!' shouted David as Minerva clung to the rigid form of Cybele in the road. 'We must get her back in, quickly!'

With beads of sweat sprouting under his pony tail, David pulled the hysterical Minerva away from her mother's corpse and hauled her up and back into the Willow coffin lying on the roadside. It was amazing the God-like strength one found in the face of adversity.

He mouthed a silent plea to the almighty while peeling a screaming Minerva away from her mother's dead body. It was a frantic and uncompromising situation to be in but life (and death in this case) with Minerva was never without its challenges.

'David! What are we going to do?!' wailed Minerva, clinging to him.

'We are going to stay calm for a start!' shouted David.

David's stomach began to churn but he would not lose control. God was right there, he was sure of it. He could feel the reassuring hand of the almighty as the scene around him spiralled from bad to worse. Carried by the wind, came the sound of someone else's cries, but this time it was the sound of hysterical laughter. And it was coming from a familiar looking couple heading down the road towards them. Gerald and Isis.

Isis was pointing and screaming with laughter at another figure on the opposite side of the road with a dog. It was Mrs. Rocket and her beloved Rune, a very old, chocolate Labrador with the oddest of gaits, paddling beside her. On further inspection, David noticed the dog was wearing the postman's hat as he continued to paddle in slow and deliberate steps beside his owner. It was a strange sight - a dog wearing a hat, a shocked owner and a screaming onlooker with a partner clearly trying to pacify her.

Is nothing sacred anymore? thought David as his eyes flitted to the corpse in front of him. 'Gerald!' David waved his arms and bellowed through the gusts of wind as it carried the screams of Minerva and Isis away and into the ether.
Gerald glanced across the road, 'David,' he boomed, 'What's going on?!'

This only seemed to infuse the situation with more hysteria, especially when Minerva and Isis recognized each other and Mrs. Rocket thought she recognized something else.

'Well I never,' she chortled, pointing to Minerva's motionless mother propped up under David's arms as he hauled her across the road, 'They're so life-like these scarecrows aren't they? Did you make that one yourself vicar?'

Minerva gave a woeful wail while Isis wailed with laughter.

'It's not what you think Mrs. Rocket,' said David, hauling Cybele back towards Mr. Morris and the coffin, 'Give us a hand would you Gerald?'

Mrs. Rocket looked as confused as her dog, 'It's not? What ever is it then...?' She stopped in mid-sentence, her eyes growing bigger, 'Oh I see, well I think I do...' she said, looking at Minerva and the Willow coffin, the lilies and the lavender.

'It's my mother you stupid woman!' shouted Minerva, arms and hair flying in all directions. 'Not a bloody scarecrow....it's my dead mother, that's who it is!'

Isis cackled loudly while poor Mrs. Rocket looked on in horror, her hand flying to her mouth as fast as the wind flew all around her. 'I'm so sorry,' she gasped, immediately making the sign of the cross. 'I didn't realize! Oh dear, what a terrible mistake to make...'

She glanced down at her dog, quickly removing the hat before crossing the road and placing it back on the scarecrow postman with quiet reverence on her way past.

'Thank you Mrs. Rocket,' said David in hushed tones. 'Very kind of you. I hope you and Rune haven't been too alarmed. This wind really is the devil in disguise isn't it?'

Mrs. Rocket didn't say a word as she turned and walked away.

'I think that might've been the last straw for the poor woman,' said David straightening his dog collar.

Gerald winked at David before joining him in an effort to re-install Minerva's mother back into the Willow basket, while Minerva and Isis chased after the scattered lilies and lavender in the road.

'What's the matter with you Isis?' said Minerva, 'You don't seem your usual self.'

'On the contrary Minerva!' shrieked Isis. 'I've found myself at last. Everything is fitting into place!'

Isis fell about in uncontrollable laughter leaving Minerva looking at Gerald, 'What have you done to her Gerald? She's not herself is she?'

'She's probably more herself than she's ever been...' said Gerald from the other side of the coffin as they were sliding it back into Mr. Morris, 'thanks to what she found in my kitchen. A certain magical supply of ingredients which found themselves into a teapot and Isis managed to drink two cupfuls of the stuff.'

'What kind of magical supply are you talking about Gerald?' said Minerva, looking serious. 'Purely organic I hope?'

'Of course Minerva, what do you take me for?'

'You're still a bit of an unknown quantity Gerald. And you can't blame me for taking an interest in my friend's welfare. She can be fragile at times, as you know, or at least I hope you do. What was in that tea?'

She watched her friend as she chased the flying lilies, leaping like a ballerina and twirling with the wind.

'Mushrooms - Liberty Caps to be precise.'

Minerva rose to full height which was exactly level with Gerald's left ear.

'Liberty Caps? repeated Minerva, 'You mean to say Isis is under the influence of magic mushrooms?'

'Is the answer my friend...' laughed Isis as she weaved backwards and forwards from one side of the road to the other.

'What —' shouted Minerva, scrambling to pick up the last of the lilies and lavender, '— are you talking about Isis?'

'Blowing in the wind...' sang Isis, 'The answer is blowing in the wind...'

'Well I'm glad you've got the answer, at least one of us knows what's going on!' said Minerva before turning to Gerald, 'Do you have any brandy on you?'

'I have a little something,' he said, pulling a small, silver hip flask from his pocket and passing it to Minerva.

'I can't believe what I'm hearing,' she said, before taking a large gulp.

'Well you'd better believe it, because it's happened,' said Gerald, glaring at her. 'Do you think I would deliberately give Isis something like that without her knowing? Especially with the funeral going on? I think not. It was a mistake, that's all.'

'That's all? *That's all?*' screamed Minerva, 'Isis is tripping on magic mushrooms and that's all? This could damage her beyond recognition Gerald and you know it!'

'No,' said Gerald, 'I don't know it because that's not the case at all Minerva. You're over reacting to something which is not harmful - not in the quantities Isis has consumed – and anyway, there's nothing we can do now but wait until they've worn off.'

'And how long will that be?'

'By the end of the day she'll be suitably chilled out I would think,' said Gerald, taking back the hip flask. 'Especially if she's had a few cocktails.'

'I hope you're right,' said Minerva, glancing over at Isis. 'She's got a way to go yet, by the look of her...'

'Trust me Minerva, she'll be fine, I shall make sure of it,' said Gerald. 'Don't worry about Isis, you have enough to think about!'

'I think we need to get a move on,' said David after wrestling with the bungee cord and the rear doors, 'There's been enough of a delay already. Do you want a lift Gerald?'

'Is there enough room for all of us?' said Gerald holding up the shoulder bag containing his drum.

'Yes I should think so,' said David. 'Can you round up Isis?'

'I'll try,' said Gerald, 'She's a bit preoccupied though.'

'Isis!' cried Minerva, taking the hip flask back from Gerald, 'As you seem to be so attached to those lilies, would you care to join them in the back of Mr. Morris for a trip up the road?'

'Not much room is there?' Isis giggled and took the hip flask from Minerva. 'But then again, we're all pieces of the puzzle aren't we? Everything fits together perfectly in the end doesn't it?'

Minerva sighed heavily, 'I'm glad you're seeing it that way. You won't mind going in the back with my mother then?'

'I could be the psychopomp!' said Isis. 'Isn't that what they do? Transport souls to their final destination?'

'They do indeed,' said Minerva, 'Are you sure you're up to it?'

'I've never felt better!' said Isis.

'You go in the front with David,' Minerva gestured to Gerald, 'I'll squash in with Isis and my mother and we shall sing her soul back home...'

'The wind's dropped,' said David looking up at a darkening

sky, 'But it looks like rain. Get in ladies and let's be on our way please!'

A flurry of activity followed as the bungee cord flew off as the doors sprang open and Minerva and Isis bundled inside.

'Oh my Goddess!' squealed Minerva, 'All my worst fears have come at once!'

'What's that?' called Isis from one side of the coffin.

'Small spaces get to me I'm afraid. I find it hard to breathe.'

'If that's true then it won't be long before we're all dead,' said Gerald in the front.

Minerva sat in stony silence. As if she hadn't suffered enough.

'You're made of stronger stuff than you think,' said Gerald still facing the dashboard.

'Isis,' proclaimed Minerva, 'Let's begin shall we? Can you remember the Dance of the Souls?'

'The song or the dance?' said Isis, peering across the coffin at Minerva.

'The song of course! I wouldn't say there's much room for dancing in here would you?'

'No!' Isis collapsed into another fit of giggles, 'Not much room at all!'

Gerald swung around sharply to stare at Isis, who completely ignored him much to Minerva's amusement. She continued to snort and giggle and as strange as her behaviour was, it did do something to lift the mood of everyone in the car.

There are elements of joy to be found at the most unexpected and oddest of times.

18

Willows and Basket Cases

Joe looked up at the sky and then at Ronnie, 'Are you sure it was 11.30?'

'Positive,' said Ronnie, 'Mum kept repeating it like a mantra. You don't forget something like that.'

'Well someone's forgotten something. We've been here over half an hour now and not a sign of them...'

Ronnie began to chew her lip, 'And Morrigan will need picking up at one. They're good at the nursery and have already agreed to have her for an extra hour but I don't want to push it.'

Joe pulled her towards the great Oak towering over them. 'We could dance round the tree if you like?'

Ronnie stared up at the huge canopy of branches. 'It's magnificent isn't it? Gran will be pleased to be in such good company.'

Joe leaned against the massive trunk and pulled out his pouch of tobacco, 'Had any more visits from the old girl?'

She stared out across the field, 'Yes, this morning when I was out walking Basil. She was as real as you are, it's getting stronger!'

'Nothing you can't handle Ron, and it's not such a bad thing is it, seeing dead people. Quite comforting really, wouldn't you say?'

'Yeah, I suppose... It doesn't scare me anymore but I just wish I knew what it's all about. What am I supposed to do with this *gift* as you put it?'

'There you go trying to work it all out. Don't even try, just accept it as a gift from those Gods your Mum's always talking about. That's as good a reason as any isn't it? The thing is Ron, all these experiences you've been having all point to the same thing: life goes on in more ways than we think.'

Ronnie thought how cool he looked, standing on one leg, one hand deep in his pocket, leaning back, one knee bent and resting on the trunk, casually drawing on his perfectly rolled cigarette.

'I know, but it's all so real to me! And just a bit unbelievable to other people right? I mean, who's going to take me seriously?'

'Does it really matter who believes you and who doesn't? I believe what's been happening to you, your mother will for sure and you'd probably be surprised how many others would too. But does it really matter what other people think? You know your own mind and you're the one having these conversations with dead people. Accept it for what it is, eh? I reckon it's all good stuff. Nothing to worry about, but that might be...look!' he pointed to the dark clouds looming in the distance.

'Oh well,' sighed Ronnie, 'Not much we can do about it is there? Gran did love the rain though, so it doesn't surprise me one bit.'

He laughed again, holding an arm out to her as the billowing smoke curled around the Oak and disappeared into the vast expanse of sky. Ronnie pressed her body into his and they stood looking out in silence. He was right about other people, what they thought was up to them. Only love mattered in the end, however corny it sounded.

Ronnie could feel her whole body charging up with energy as they slipped into silence, drinking in the view of the open field and surrounding farmland. The sound of their own breathing and the tweeting and humming of birds and insects was followed by the stillness that often heralds a coming shower or storm.

Or a car.

'Isn't that the Morris?' Joe pointed at something in the distance. 'Over there Ron!'

Ronnie narrowed her eyes, 'You're right, it is. But I don't understand, they were all supposed to be coming in a hearse.'

'Well that's a strange looking hearse if ever I saw one! Unless, hang on... who else is that in the car?'

Ronnie peered over his shoulder as Mr. Morris rumbled closer towards them along the unmade track, 'Oh crikey,' she groaned, 'Gran's in the back by the looks of it, with Mum and Isis.'

'And that's David and Gerald in the front,' said Joe, 'David's driving.'

'He's doing the service too,' said Ronnie, 'So I'm not surprised he's in the driver's seat.'

'So it's a bit of a cocktail of a funeral then?' A Pagan style burial with a Christian twist?'

'You could say that. The best of both worlds, Mum said, but then again, by the look of things, anything could happen or maybe *has* happened...'

'And we're just about to find out,' said Joe, as Mr. Morris bounced to a halt in front of the Oak tree.

* * *

After a bumpy landing and dis-embarkment of all passengers, there was a flurry of further activity while the Willow basket and Cybele were carefully removed and laid beneath the great boughs of the Oak. Hair was patted down, dog collars straightened, drums set into place and lilies and lavender rearranged for the last time. All eyes were on David as he searched his pockets for the reading he'd so carefully written and pulled out a bingo card instead.

'What's the matter David?' Minerva tightened her grip on a swaying Isis.

David continued his search, 'I could have sworn I had it.'

'What?'

'My words. The service was all prepared. I always write down what I want to say.'

'Looks like you're going to have to wing it,' said Joe squeezing Ronnie's arm. 'I do it all the time at gigs!'

'Can you remember any of it?' said Minerva, holding her hand out at the first spots of rain.

'I shall have to,' said David, straightening his jacket.

'Just let me know when to start...' said Gerald, setting his drum straight on its strap.

'Should have brought my guitar if I'd known,' whispered Joe into Ronnie's ear.

'Minerva, will you let me go!' cried Isis.

Minerva released her grip as Isis set off from the huddled group like a firework and began to dance around the tree.

'She can't go far,' said Gerald.

Minerva glared at him, 'She's far gone enough already, I think that's fairly obvious.'

'What's the matter with her?' said Ronnie.

'Mushrooms,' snapped Minerva, 'Magic ones.'

'And good one's at that,' said Gerald, 'Pure as the earth they came from.'

Joe laughed, 'Get away! Isis on mushies? Where'd you get those from Gerald?'

'They grow in abundance in the woods behind my bungalow...seems a shame not to pick them.'

'I'll have to pop round for a brew sometime,' said Joe.

Ronnie elbowed him, looking from David to her mother and back again.

David clasped his hands loosely together and cleared his throat, 'Can we just take a moment to be quiet?'

As far as Isis was concerned, there was no quiet about it. In between hopping and skipping, she sang at the top of her voice and mostly to the tree while the rest of the party did their best to humour and ignore her at the same time.

David spoke in soft, dulcet tones and Minerva noticed how different he looked as he took on the role of priest; his presence alone commanding a hushed silence from all present – apart from Isis, who continued to whoop and holler like a cheerleader at a baseball game.

Minerva couldn't ever remember anyone saying such nice things about her mother before now and for a moment wondered if it was the same person he was so fondly recollecting. Pity that she had to die to have such good things said about her.

The sound of his voice lulled her into a warm cocoon as her eyes wandered over the Willow coffin and back over David's body in quick succession. She shifted her position but couldn't ignore the spark rekindling inside. What had made her choose

Willow? It wasn't as if it was her mother's favourite tree. She thought of the boomerang still there on the mantelpiece, alongside the red candle and the black garter. The power of magic and the profound timing of the Goddess never ceased to amaze her. Her whole body was sizzling with the heat of something familiar and it wasn't a hot flush.

David looked at her, the hint of a smile teasing the corner of his lips, 'Shall we do it now?'

She could feel his warm breath on her neck, 'Oh yes please...' she said.

'Are you sure? Is it deep enough?'

'I'm sure it will be...'

'Mum! Are you okay?'

Ronnie's voice jolted her back to the four pairs of eyes on her.

'Oh, said Minerva, 'What did you say David?'

David pointed to the Willow basket, 'I said it's time to lay your mother to rest now and just wondered if the hole looked a bit shallow. There's a couple of extra spades over there in the shed. You're a gardener, Gerald, what do you think?'

Gerald peered over the coffin, 'Plenty of room in there, David. I think we're safe...no grave robbers round these parts.'

Ronnie gasped, 'Oh Gerald, what a horrible thought!'

'A cold and dark and dirty tomb...' sang Isis as she twirled around the tree, 'A warm and sticky bloody womb...'

'Isis!' shrieked Minerva, 'That's enough! You look and sound like that awful creature in Lord of the Rings. Snap out of it! We are burying my mother and as awful as she was, she deserves some respect.'

David gave the nod to Joe who helped him lower the Willow basket slowly and carefully downwards. Gerald picked up his drum, and to the pulsing of a slow heartbeat Cybele began her decent back into the womb of Mother Earth.

It was a moving spectacle.

Minerva and Ronnie held onto each other while Isis swayed to the dull thudding of the drum. Ronnie watched a hazy light rise up from the coffin as an electric current surged through her body while Minerva watched the Willow yielding and pushing its way deep into the earth.

And David watched Minerva.

Even in mourning, she was a splendid sight…all heaving bosom and flushed skin. A Goddess right there in the flesh.

Minerva could feel David's eyes on her and warm beads of sweat pricking her cleavage. Yes, it was all coming back…the stirrings and the sensations she never thought she would feel again. Which was all very well, but not altogether appropriate given the time and place. Her mother's graveside would have been the last place for her lost libido to return, surely? There didn't seem to be any proper sense of occasion with these things at all.

'Hadn't we ought to cover her up now?' Minerva said to no one in particular.

Ronnie prompted Joe with a look and a prod in the direction of the spare spade and Gerald and Joe began to work in tandem, casting clods of fresh earth upon Cybele and the Willow basket until both had disappeared completely.

'Beats ending up in a jar, I suppose…' said Minerva, staring at the mound covering her mother. 'Beneath a mighty Oak too, it doesn't get any better than that, does it Ron?'

Ronnie wiped her eyes and managed a watery smile, 'Not if you say so Mum. I didn't know Gran liked Oaks…'

'No, she didn't like trees at all, said they got in the way. I'm sure it was something to do with my father building a treehouse for her sister, years ago. Aunt Crow got in the way, I think is the more likely story. Whatever it was, as far as trees were concerned, it left her scarred for life and the arrival of the black dog was the only thing to keep her mind off it.'

'Black dog?'

'Didn't I ever tell you? That thing was the bane of my teenage years…' Minerva shuddered at the memory, 'Not only did I have a bed-ridden mother mired in misery to care for but an invisible black dog too.'

'You mean it wasn't real?' said Ronnie.

'Oh it was real enough to her all right,' said Minerva, surveying the freshly dug mound of earth. 'Anyway it's all in the past now, dead and buried. Let's leave it there shall we? Would you mind taking Isis and Gerald back, darling?'

'No, of course not. I'll put the sausage rolls in the oven and get the glasses out ready.'

Minerva hugged her daughter, 'David and I could just do with some time to ourselves that's all…we won't be far behind you.'

'I've got it all in hand, Mum, you take your time!' called Ronnie, before attempting to herd a straying Isis and the two grave diggers into a vehicle.

Minerva and David stood in silence as the land rover rumbled away from them in a whirl of brown dust. David squeezed Minerva's hand, 'Are we about ready for the 'wake'?' he said in a gentle voice. 'I think perhaps it's time…'

There was no perhaps about it as far as Minerva was concerned. And now was definitely the time for something. What she wanted was David, and she knew he felt the same by the way he blew down his dog collar as he hurried towards

Mr. Morris.

'Talking of 'wakes', I think something is awake in me at last,' said Minerva, with a smouldering look in his direction. 'It's come back, just like the boomerang did.'

'The boomerang?' said David, blowing hard against his reddening neck.

'Yes,' purred Minerva, 'I never stopped believing you know.'

'In boomerangs?'

'Something like that...'

Minerva smiled to herself as she pulled a damp and crumpled envelope from her sweating cleavage.

'What's that?' said David, his eyes wandering from the paper to where it had been and back again.

'Oh it was something I thought I'd lost,' said Minerva, feeling the same bubble of excitement at the sight of her own magical words.

'And you found it again?' said David, loosening his dog collar.

'Oh I think so, but I could do with some extra assistance, just to confirm it.'

She touched his cheek. It was warm and waxy, 'You're getting a bit hot under the collar vicar.'

'Yes,' said David, slightly out of breath. 'After everyone's gone, I am at your service, Madam, but until then, we have a wake to get through...'

'We have the journey home to get through first...,' said Minerva with a wicked gleam in her eye, 'Isis and Gerald are gone.'

'You mean we're alone,' said David, fumbling with the car keys.

Minerva nodded slowly, 'Mr. Morris won't tell either...he's very good at keeping secrets.'

'Of course he is,' said David. 'Is there no one who escapes your magical charms, Minerva?'

She laughed, 'I can't think why they'd want to, can you, vicar?'

Silence was the only thing to come between them because there was nothing else to say. Only to do what had to be done. Magical timing is like that...it waits for no man, Witch *or* vicar. It just turns up and proclaims itself for there is little anyone can do to stop it. And Minerva and David were no exception much to one another's delight in the accommodating interior of Mr. Morris.

Minerva thought how they'd created the most divine and hallowed space there under the canopy of the Oak tree - as close to nature (and her mother) as anyone could be – and what better way to celebrate life and love than in the making of it?

The circle of life had gone around and was coming around.

All was definitely not lost.

Afterword

I hope you enjoyed the story as much as I loved writing it. If you have a couple of minutes to leave an honest review on Amazon – just a few words would be great – I'd really appreciate it!

Book 3 - Chaos in the Cauldron - releases July 2019.
'Minerva needs a holiday.
She's done battling with her dead mother's black dog.
House sitting at Spellstead Hall is the perfect remedy although Aunt Crow's pets aren't quite what Minerva and Isis are expecting...
A host of fantastical beasts including llamas, Spit and Polish, and Brenda the pot-bellied pig provide challenges galore but at least they're alive.
When things start to horribly wrong, Minerva is faced with the biggest challenge of all. Can she manage to turn it around with magic?
And more importantly, will it happen before Aunt Crow gets back?'

For news, updates on future books and a free copy of the prequel (Black Dogs and Broomsticks) to my Madness and Magic series - sign up for the Treehouse Magic Newsletter.
www.sheenacundy.com

About the Author

Songwriter. Storyteller. Sheena Cundy is a teacher of horse and rider, reader of the Tarot and a Reiki Master.

Since childhood, my love of horses and the healing and magical arts has never waned and continues to filter into my writing any which way it can.

The Madness and the Magic is the debut novel I wrote to keep out of prison, a straitjacket and the divorce courts while battling with murderous tendencies and all kinds of hormonal horrors during a mid-life crisis. Bonkers and Broomsticks is the follow up...

Apart from Witch Lit and other magical fiction, I also write spiritual non-fiction and sing and write the songs for my pagan band, ***Morrigans Path.***

You can connect with me on:

- https://sheenacundy.com
- https://twitter.com/OrgSheena
- https://www.facebook.com/SheenaCundyAuthor
- https://morriganspath.bandcamp.com
- https://www.instagram.com/treehouse_witch

Subscribe to my newsletter:

- https://www.subscribepage.com/blackdogs

Printed in Great Britain
by Amazon

38205534R00121